SHIKAMARU

T0014287

COVER + INTERIOR DESIGN Shawn Carrico
TRANSLATION Jocelyne Allen

Published by VIZ Media, LLC
P.O. Box 77010
San Francisco, CA 94107

Library of Congress Control Number: 2020951625

Printed in the U.S.A.
First Printing, March 2021

viz.com

CONTENTS

CHARACTERS

NARA SHIKADAI
Shikamaru and Temari's son. Loves video games.

NARA SHIKAMARU
Advisor to the Seventh Hokage. Former member of Team 10, Shikadai's father.

NARA TEMARI
Shikadai's mother. Older sister of the Fifth Kazekage, Gaara.

AKIMICHI CHOJI
User of the Art of Expansion. Former member of Team 10, member of Ino-Shika-Cho.

YAMANAKA INO
User of Mind Transmission jutsu. Former member of Team 10, member of Ino-Shika-Cho.

RO
Anbu shinobi. Able to change the amount and nature of chakra.

SOKU
Anbu shinobi. Skilled at fighting using chakra needles.

UZUMAKI NARUTO
The Seventh Hokage. The hero of Konohagakure. Former member of Team 7.

UZUMAKI BORUTO
Naruto's son, Sasuke's student.

UCHIHA SASUKE
User of the Uchiha Clan Sharingan. Former member of Team 7.

DARUI
Fifth Raikage. Has a habit of saying "drab."

GAARA
Fifth Kazekage. Temari's younger brother, Shikadai's uncle.

CHOJURO
Sixth Mizukage. User of the ninja sword Hirameikarei.

KUROTSUCHI
Fourth Tsuchikage. Granddaughter of the Third Tsuchikage, Ohnoki.

MADOKA IKKYU
Feudal lord of the Land of Fire. Has a strong influence in other countries as well.

SECRET SCHEMES

SHIKAMARU'S STORY: MOURNING CLOUDS

1

He woke up just like always. No matter how late he went to bed the night before, he always woke up at the same time. This habit hadn't changed from his days at the academy when he was a kid.

"Haah." Shikamaru yawned, staring up at the familiar ceiling. "Hm?"

There was an unusual scent in the air. He sniffed at his clothes to find they were permeated with the smell of fried meat and cigarette smoke and remembered that he'd stayed out late drinking with Choji the night before, something he hadn't done in a while. By the time he'd gotten home, it was the middle of the night, and naturally, Temari and Shikadai had long since gone to bed. But changing his clothes was far too much hassle, so he'd simply taken off his jacket and rolled onto his futon. Before he knew it, it was morning.

"I didn't take a bath," he muttered.

Most likely, the tub was still full of water, cold by now, of course. Thoughtful Temari. Even though she hadn't known when he'd be home, she had no doubt heated plenty of water and put the lid on the tub to keep it warm for him to enjoy later. And now that he was thinking about it, he was pretty sure supper had been laid out for him on the kitchen table, covered in a cloth.

"Aaw, crap." Choji's invitation had been so sudden, he'd forgotten to tell Temari. He covered his face with his arm. "What a drag."

The fact that he hadn't called, the fact that he hadn't gotten in the bath, the fact that he'd fallen asleep in his clothes—it was all entirely on him. He thought of all the things he'd soon have to say: *I know. I know it's all my fault. You don't have to tell me...*

"Dammit!" He yanked himself up into a sitting position. His head was clear, at least. No ninja could drink so much it would have an effect on them the next day.

Cold water or not, it was time to get in that bath. He slapped his cheeks a couple times to psych himself up. His hair was still tied back, but stray hairs were poking out all over the place thanks to all the tossing and turning he'd done in his sleep. The ends of these drooping hairs stabbed annoyingly into his forehead. He undid the tie to release his hair and shook his head furiously from side to side.

"Woh-kay!" He tried to cheer himself on, but his heart was still heavy. He opened the sliding door and stepped out into the hallway, startling his son, Shikadai, who looked up at him with wide eyes.

"M-morning," Shikamaru said, his voice hoarse.

"You got a cold?" Shikadai asked, his sharp gaze too much like that of his mother.

"Nah, just talked a little too much yesterday."

Choji always raised his voice when he was drinking, so Shikamaru also ended up talking more loudly in order to hold up his end of the conversation without being drowned out. Plus, he smoked more because he was enjoying himself, so a night out like that inevitably put an extra burden on his throat.

"Hey, Dad?" Shikadai whispered, leaning forward to bring his face in close. "Mom's in a pretty bad mood this morning."

Shikamaru could have guessed that, just as he could have guessed that the cause of that bad mood was his own self.

He could hear the sound of chopping on the cutting board from the kitchen down the hallway and past the living room. It was much more violent than usual. She was pretty angry.

"Sounds like." He smiled bitterly.

Shikadai bumped him with his shoulder. "Good luck."

His son sounded so grown-up now. It felt like only last week that he was bursting into tears at the slightest fall. With his tied-back hair, Shikadai looked so much like Shikamaru, especially from above.

He tousled the boy's head fiercely.

"Stop it. You'll get cigarette stink on me."

"Quiet, you. Don't get all cheeky with me. Go to work. You got some attention with the chunin exams, so I know you're getting harder missions these days. Unless you focus, you'll only be holding your teammates back."

Now that he thought about it, it was the chunin exams that had gotten people paying attention to *him* too. The exams were also where he'd met Temari for the first time. Enemies when they met, married now. You never knew what would happen in life.

"You eat breakfast?" he asked his son.

"Yeah."

"You're all set?"

"Pretty much," Shikadai replied, rolling his eyes.

"So then get going already." Shikamaru reached for his son's hair again, but Shikadai ducked away.

"I *am*."

"Good luck."

"Honestly. What a drag." Shikadai glanced at Shikamaru with reproachful eyes and then headed out the front door.

Kid seriously reminds me of a certain someone...

Himself, of course. Shikadai didn't just look like his dad when he was younger; he grumbled like him, too.

"Now then."

Shikamaru took a few deep breaths, then went into the kitchen.

"'Morning," he said to his wife's back. She didn't turn around. "I'm gonna jump in the bath."

He got no answer. Which was only natural.

With a heavy heart, he reheated the bath and got in, lost in thought. How much yelling was he in for exactly? Or would he get the silent treatment for a few days? Just thinking about it made his stomach shrink into itself.

He got out of the bath and dried off carefully. *Changing clothes is such a drag*, he thought. He opened the bathroom door to find a stack of freshly washed and neatly folded work clothes before him. Slipping his arms through the sleeves of the shirt, he picked up the jacket in one hand and headed to the living room.

Temari was sitting on the floor in her usual place at the low table. Warm rice and miso soup were laid out together with fried fish where Shikamaru sat. The usual Nara family breakfast.

He sat down quietly.

"Sorry about yesterday," he said with a smile to his silent wife, who had her eyes lowered.

At times like this, the best thing to do was to simply apologize. If he tried to offer up excuses, all he would get in return were a myriad of counterattacks. This was Shikamaru's secret to success, cultivated through long years of married life.

"Thanks for breakfast." He clapped his hands together in thanks and picked up his chopsticks. He took a sip of miso soup and dug into the rice. "This is great."

First, compliment her. He had to focus on at least not making his wife's mood any worse. The whole thing was his fault. He would show her how wholly sorry he was.

Normally, she would have said something to reproach him by now, but her mood was apparently worse than usual this morning.

Why?

Stinking of smoke, falling asleep without getting in the bath, not eating supper, forgetting to call her—it had all happened any number of times before. So then why today, now of all times, was she this angry?

Although he'd complimented her on the breakfast he was shoveling down, he couldn't actually taste a bite of it; he was too focused on his wife sitting silently beside him. He finished half of the fried fish and started in on the other side. His rice was almost gone.

"More rice?" Temari finally spoke.

"Please." He smiled and held out his bowl.

Temari refused to meet his gaze as she accepted the bowl and piled fresh rice into it. "Here."

"Thanks." On a normal day, he would accept the bowl without a word, but today, he thanked her without thinking.

"Um," he said, digging into the fresh rice. He didn't actually have anything in particular to say, but he knew he should say something.

Temari beat him to the punch. "Do you remember what day yesterday was?" she asked, her voice thorny.

Shikamaru felt an arrow of ice shoot through his heart.

Oh crap!

Their wedding anniversary. He had forgotten right up
until that very second. With all the clean-up work after the
remaining members of the Otsutsuki clan had crashed Shikadai's
chunin exams and the preparations for the Five Kage Summit in a
few days, it had completely slipped his mind.

He set his chopsticks down and lowered his head so
swiftly that he nearly slammed his forehead into the table.

"I'm sorry!"

"You forgot."

"I'm so, so sorry!"

Temari's gaze was sharp, like the tip of an icicle. A cold
sweat broke out on Shikamaru's face.

"I know you're busy as Naruto's advisor, so I won't say
too much really," she said. "But yesterday, at the very least,
I would have liked it if you could have had supper at home."

"I will definitely make this up to you."

"I'm gone forever if yesterday happens again."

"I know. But it definitely won't!"

"You'll be late for work. You have to get ready for the meeting
of the Five Kages, don't you?"

She was right. He needed to head out pretty soon, so he
quickly put the rest of his breakfast in his belly and stood up.

Temari started to clear away the dishes.

"I'm really sorry. Forgive me."

"You're going to be late." She turned her back on him in
the kitchen.

"I'll get going then."

Outside, he walked, shoulders slumped, along the road that
led to the Hokage Residence. He looked up at the sky and let out
a sigh. Snowy white clouds drifted from west to east.

"Family," he muttered. "What a drag."

2

Right from the start, Shikamaru was tense. The mood in the room was different from usual. Standing behind Naruto, who was seated at the center of the round table, he stared hard at the cause of this strange aura.

Kurotsuchi...

A young ninja, she had inherited the position of Tsuchikage, the leader of the Iwagakure ninja, from her grandfather Ohnoki. Peeking out from beneath her short hair, her eyes had had a hard edge to them since the start of the summit, and now they were turned squarely on Naruto.

As Naruto pretended not to notice this piercing gaze, he explained what had happened when the chunin exams had been interrupted and the aftermath of the attack on Konoha by Otsutsuki Momoshiki and his gang. Naruto had been abducted in that attack, and the Kages from the other great villages had banded together to rescue him. Naturally, the Tsuchikage Kurotsuchi had also been part of that mission. Gaara of Sunagakure, Chojuro of Kirigakure, and Darui of Kumogakure had joined Kurotsuchi and Naruto in the group known as the Five Kages, the shinobi who were the pinnacle of the ninja world in every part of the continent.

When the Fourth Great Ninja War broke out, it wasn't only ninja who were dragged into the conflict, but all the people living on the continent. The villages the Five Kages ruled over had joined forces and fought together. The friendship they had built during that time continued even after the great war ended. This was a first in the long history of ninja—the great nations, once split into fighting factions, had managed to forge a relationship based on peace.

The linchpin in this was without a doubt Naruto, the hero

who brought about the end of the Fourth Great Ninja War. His enormous power and optimistic, upbeat personality had brought together the other Kages and the ninja of the villages they controlled.

"So that's basically it. Sorry for all the hassle. Real piece of work this time. We're gonna do everything we can to make sure nothing like this happens again. Believe it." Naruto scratched the back of his head and bowed to the four Kages.

Naruto's good friend Kazekage Gaara, eyes rimmed with dark circles, nodded his acceptance of this apology.

"Coulda been a lot worse. And we're all fine. No need to bow your head like that," Raikage Darui said languidly, pushing back against his seat.

Mizukage Chojuro shrugged. "At any rate, if you detect any other strange happenings, please report them to us right away."

"Got it," Naruto said. "I'll let you know straight away if anything else comes up. I'm really sorry about all the trouble."

"If 'sorry' was enough, we wouldn't need ninja." Kurotsuchi's cold voice sliced through the air as though to wipe Naruto's grin off of his face.

"I-I said I was sorry." Naruto bowed his head again under Kurotsuchi's glare.

"These things always, *always* happen with the village of Konohagakure at the center. We only ever learn of the situation once things have gotten so bad that we have no choice but to get involved."

"This kind of thing doesn't happen *that* often—"

"How long do you intend to placate us like this?! When will you stop toying with us, Konoha?!" Kurotsuchi slammed a hand down on the white table.

"Hey, aren't you a little too hot under the collar today,

Kurotsuchi?" Darui glanced at her out of the corner of his eye and clasped his hands behind his head. Alongside Chojuro and Shikamaru, they had come up together as comrades, a group that comprised ninja working toward the next generation of the five great nations. Shikamaru's wife, Temari, had also been one of their members back then.

Ignoring Darui, Kurotsuchi continued to glare at Naruto. "I simply cannot overlook the incident at the chunin exams."

"I said I was sorry about the trouble," the Hokage insisted again.

"This isn't about Otsutsuki," she snapped.

Naruto froze, a stiff smile still on his lips. Beads of cold sweat trickled down his forehead.

Shikamaru couldn't remember anyone getting this heated at a meeting of the Five Kages since he'd started attending them. Kurotsuchi's blood was boiling on this particular day.

"The tool your son used." Her glare grew even icier. "You mind telling us about that?"

The scientific ninja tools…

Jutsu was printed on small scrolls and that ejected from a band wrapped around the wrist, which allowed anyone to use all kinds of extremely difficult techniques. Katasuke, the leader of the scientific ninja tool team, had developed this new technology. In order to appeal to the wider community for its use in actual battle, he had persuaded Naruto's son, Boruto, to use it during the chunin exam. With this tool anyone could use Naruto's Rasengan, Sasuke's Chidori, or Shikamaru's Kageshibari—which meant the skill and value of the individual ninja's potency would be diminished if not lost completely. After all, it was only after constant training that a ninja was able to discover their own personal jutsu. This was precisely why each ninja was extremely particular about their own techniques. It was only natural; the crystallization of their personal ninja path was this very jutsu. It wasn't something for just anyone to go and use.

Shikamaru remained silent and stared at Kurotsuchi.

The Tsuchikage stood up and glared at Naruto, her hands still on the table. "What exactly was Konoha thinking developing something like that in secret?"

"O-oh, the scientific ninja team was just—"

"Why do you intend to pacify us with excuses?!"

Most likely, Kurotsuchi had come to the meeting planning to attack Naruto. She clearly intended to destroy him this time. Her firm resolve was the cause the strange tension in the room, the unpleasant aura that had been assaulting Shikamaru's senses.

Every word she was saying had likely been carefully scripted, which meant they were still in the early stages of this game. Kurotsuchi moved her pieces deftly, but her attack was too single-minded, harping on a single note. She was coming at them with every piece she had straight out of the gate, not waiting for them to make a single move. If they kept listening without speaking, Kurotsuchi would reveal what she was really after soon enough.

Crossing his arms to hide his black-gloved fists, Shikamaru watched the meeting unfold.

"If that guy with the glasses hadn't stepped in, we would never have found out about these ninja tools. The other villages only learned of them because of his vanity. So who's to say that Konoha isn't developing other techniques in secret?"

"E-every village is working out ways to make life better," Naruto protested desperately.

"We're not talking about a useful tool here. This is a *weapon*. I can't just sit here and say nothing like the rest of you when I think about a tool like that being perfected and given to all the ninja in Konoha." Kurotsuchi glanced at the other

Kages. "After all, this thing could make a genin into a Naruto. With that technology strapped to their wrist, pretty much anyone could lash out with jutsu on par with Kekkei Genkai."

Normally, ninja possessed a chakra of only a single nature, but the chakras of people with Kekkei Genkai contained two or more natures. Thus, they were able to use jutsu the average person could not, even after laborious training. Kekkei Genkai were the wall that separated the average from the extraordinary.

"Why would you need to develop a ninja tool like that?" The corners of Kurotsuchi's lips curled up slightly.

Faced with this ruthless smile, Naruto gulped audibly.

"Konoha is—" Kurotsuchi began.

"You mind if I say something?" Shikamaru interrupted. Raising a hand, he looked at the Five Kages.

Kurotsuchi's eyes glittered black as she glared at him. He had clearly jumped in at the very moment she had prepared to strike a critical blow.

I'm not going to stand here and let you pin him down, Shika-maru thought.

"Developing ninja tools is something every village does," he said. "And it's also perfectly natural for people to try and make progress, to move forward every day. If we were planning some evil use for this technology as the Tsuchikage is implying, then yes, it would indeed be extremely dangerous. But it an also be used for peaceful purposes. First of all, it's no easy feat to seal a powerful jutsu in one of these scrolls. And if you're worried the young ones'll stop training because of this ninja tool, well, that's something else altogether. But don't you think it's a pretty big leap to simply assume it'll be used for military reasons?"

"Shikamaru here's right. We're talking about a child's toy. It can't compete with real jutsu." Darui smiled as he looked over at Shikamaru. He might have been a ninja from another village, but he was a comrade, and the two of them had spent long years talking passionately about the future of ninja. The bond Shikamaru felt with him was no different than if they had been from the same village.

"Is it really okay, though?" Chojuro said, propping his elbows up on the table and covering the lower half of his face with his clasped hands.

"What are you trying to say?" Gaara asked.

"What if one country gets the jump on the others while we're all being chummy?" Chojuro continued, looking at the Kazekage out of the corner of his eye. "And which country happens to be closest to getting a hold of such power that none of the others would have a chance against them?"

"What exactly are you getting at, Chojuro?" Naruto asked, perplexed, sweat beading on his forehead.

Chojuro had always taken a friendly position when it came to Konoha. This was the first time he'd ever agreed with anything like what Kurotsuchi was saying now. But Shikamaru could see what was behind this shift.

Kirigakure had remarkably little in the way of the mineral resources essential for ninja—not only the iron and copper they used for a variety of things, but also the saltpeter needed for gunpowder. Soon after the five great nations established friendly relations, economic treaties were established that gave Kirigakure access to Iwagakure minerals in exchange for quality water resources.

Kurotsuchi had to have been making her move now in some kind of secret agreement with Chojuro. It was easy for Shikamaru to accept the other ninja's change of heart when he thought about it like this. Countries couldn't run on feelings alone, after all.

Shikamaru also noticed the deep furrow carved into

the Mizukage's brow, which in addition to attempting to shroud the rest of his face with his hands, revealed his inner conflict.

"What exactly is going on with you two? I told you before, I'll make sure to tell you right away if anything comes up. Trust me. This kinda thing won't happen again," Naruto pleaded as he looked back and forth between the two Kages.

Konoha's military might was by far the greatest of the five hidden villages. The negotiations might go a little more smoothly if they acknowledged that power. But Naruto would never concede to that. He always treated everyone as an equal and despised the idea of using force to makee others yield. It was precisely because of this humble trait that Shikamaru had absolute faith in Naruto. However, this same trait was also what made Naruto a bit unreliable at times like this.

Telling himself that this was also one of Naruto's charms, Shikamaru kept his eyes focused on the round table.

"Sasuke was working behind the scenes on the whole thing with Otsutsuki, right?" Kurotsuchi asked. "His crimes were so great that no one would've batted an eye if he'd been locked up at Hozuki Castle for the rest of his life. And as his good friend, you would also know that his escape was part of what led to the Fourth Great Ninja War."

"We dealt with all that ages ago." When it came to Sasuke, Naruto couldn't keep his cool. Kurotsuchi was indeed correct in saying that Uchiha Sasuke was a major criminal and a trigger for the great war. But that same war would never have ended without Sasuke. This monumental achievement balanced out his crime of desertion, and in the end, he'd been given probation, which is where the Five Kages' discussion on this topic had ended. Naruto was perfectly correct in noting that now.

Even so, Kurotsuchi pursued it tenaciously. "Konoha still

keeps the man who tried to destroy the world. And not only that, you allow him to wander the continent, reporting on countries. A spy like that—"

"One more quick word?" Shikamaru raised a hand. And then without waiting for assent from anyone, he began speaking. "Reconnaissance is a requisite for ninja. Again, this isn't just about Konoha. All the villages regularly visit the other villages in secret. We don't reproach each other for that, and if anyone is discovered doing this sort of work, we don't call for the death penalty. The ninja who's arrested is made to return any information obtained and then promptly released. That's one of the principles of this alliance. The other villages agreed that Naruto would take responsibility for Sasuke. Even if, as the Tsuchikage is implying, Konoha *were* using Sasuke to maneuver in the other countries with the intention of using the scientific ninja tools to carry out an invasion at some point, would this all go exactly according to Konoha's plan? The answer is no. None of the villages on the continent would forgive Konoha for scrapping the sacred alliance our predecessors worked to build. No matter how strong Konoha might be, we couldn't win against the other great nations and all the smaller countries. It's a deterrent against anyone running off on their own. Isn't that the point of the alliance we have?"

Eyes closed, Darui nodded several times. Gaara was also silent, his arms folded. Chojuro lowered his gaze, brow still furrowed, and looked away from Shikamaru, while Kurotsuchi glared at him, gritting her teeth.

"You will not deceive me with fancy speeches." She pushed each word out from behind clenched teeth.

Should be nearing the end of the uproar soon...

Shikamaru stared at Kurotsuchi and waited.

Her pale slender arms beat at the table. She raised a hand

and turned her index finger toward Naruto. "Konoha has too many secrets. Because you're a powerful country, you're going to have to show some good faith at least if you intend to work in harmony with the rest of us. To back up your promise to never let these sorts of things happen again, I demand the disclosure of Konoha's classified information."

"Wha—" Naruto stiffened, at a loss for words.

Shikamaru crossed his arms and leaned back against the wall.

Disclosure of classified information...

Did she intend to strip Konoha naked?

"If this demand is not met, I cannot say that Iwagakure won't withdraw from the alliance."

"I'd like some time to think about this, too." Chojuro followed Kurotsuchi.

"We'll hear your answer at the next meeting." Kurotsuchi shot a glare at Shikamaru before leaving the room, and Chojuro and their aides chased after her.

"H-hey! Hang on a minute..." Naruto said lifelessly, rising up out of his seat.

"What a drag," Shikamaru grumbled, still leaning against the wall.

3

"Been a while since I saw you two," Shikamaru said to his old friends in his own office next to the Hokage's.

Before him stood two ninja wearing white masks, one a monkey and the other a cat. From their physical statures, it was clear that the monkey was a man and the cat a woman.

"Totally. Like, ages," the woman said, removing her mask. Her orange hair, once long, was now cut short. When they'd met, she was a girl just out of the academy, but the intervening decade had turned the girl into a woman. Her eyes, looking down on Shikamaru sitting at his desk, were brimming with confidence. As an Anbu commander, she'd come through countless bloody battles.

"You still all 'like, like,' huh, Hinoko?"

"It's not something you can, like, just stop just 'cause someone told you to. And, like, I told you before not to call me by my real name!"

"I guess you did, Hinoko."

"Gah! You, like, just said it again!"

Shikamaru's lips curled up at the familiar exchange. Hinoko's Anbu name was Soku. She hated her real name and got angry when called by it. Shikamaru was well aware of this fact, but he did it anyway.

"You must calm yourself," sighed the man in the monkey mask. He removed his mask to reveal a stern jaw and thick eyebrows. The hair that was black in Shikamaru's memories was threaded with conspicuous gray now. Going by the name of Ro, he was a veteran ninja, a dozen or so years older than Shikamaru.

Shikamaru had once been assigned to work with them for a period. He would never forget it: the Land of Silence.

When all communication ceased with Sai, who had gone to this small country to find Gengo, a man who could control people with words alone, Shikamaru had, without saying a word to anyone, set out on the journey to the Land of Silence to find him alongside these two Anbu ninja. He had been captured and very nearly caught in Gengo's trap when Temari came to his rescue and awakened him from the vocal genjutsu. It was all a fond memory now. That had been the first and last time he'd worked as part of a three-person cell with the Anbu.

Currently, both Ro and Soku were jonin leading their own squads. But peace had come to the world, and so the Anbu had also seen their numbers in steady decline. Ninja like these two, able at work on the front lines, were valuable resources. Shikamaru had half-forced their schedules open to bring them before him now.

This was an important matter. He wanted to leave it to people he could trust.

"Lord Shikamaru is, at present, second-in-command in Konoha. Tread lightly with him, or you will be *sec-olded* harshly." Ro pursed his lips as he distinctly emphasized "scolded."

Raising an eyebrow, Shikamaru looked at Hinoko. "This old guy still the same as ever?"

"I think he was, like, making a play on 'second' and 'scold,'" Hinoko said, looking exasperated, and Ro listened with a tense smile. This middle-aged ninja had a habit of making bad puns and jokes.

Although Shikamaru had remembered that Hinoko got angry when she heard her real name, he'd forgotten Ro's pun thing, but it all came back to him when he saw his look of self-satisfaction. He hadn't understood Ro's pun at all, but naturally Hinoko had caught on instantly. But even now that he knew what the pun was meant to be, it wasn't funny at all. Still, he rewarded Ro's efforts with a wry smile.

"Coming together after all this time means some kind of annoying job, right?" Hinoko asked, a serious look on her face.

"Mm." Shikamaru brought his gloved hand to his mouth. He stared at the Anbu. "Smells like fire around Mount Iwa. I want you to go check into how much magma we're looking at."

"Oh ho!" Ro knit his thick eyebrows together.

As for Hinoko, a smile spread across lips painted in orange lipstick. They knew just from the words "Mount Iwa" that he was talking about Iwagakure. "Haven't, like, heard anything 'on fire' in a while," she said, brushing back her short front fringe with orange nails.

It was true that since the Great Ninja War—no, since the Five Kages joined hands—fighting between countries had dropped dramatically. They were, of course, different communities, so smaller conflicts were an everyday occurrence, but because they all prioritized cooperation, none of these had ever turned into anything more serious.

Which was exactly why when it started to come apart at the seams, the whole thing would burst open. Stability bred inflexibility, and inflexibility made swift reaction impossible. A single sharp and powerful shock was all that was needed to cause one tiny fragment after the other to chip away, revealing the peace they believed in to be nothing more than an illusion. He had to pluck this budding unrest out at the root sooner than later.

"Was there some matter of concern at the earlier meeting?" Ro asked. His intuition was as sharp as ever.

Shikamaru nodded. "The Tsuchikage proposed a strange motion."

"Which was?"

"Disclosure of Konoha's confidential information to the other villages."

"Ha! There's, like, no way you can do that. We're hidden villages precisely 'cause we got secrets. That's not, like, something a ninja working in the shadows'd say."

Hinoko was exactly right. As someone who governed a village, Kurotsuchi was proposing something well beyond the realm of common sense. Exposing the secrets of their own country was equivalent to admitting defeat as a village. Kurotsuchi was not a stupid woman. She had said what she said in full awareness of this.

Why exactly? Shikamaru couldn't get past how odd the whole thing was. Kurotsuchi's move was far too reckless. There had to be something behind it. If he were Kurotsuchi…

Disturbance. Dare to make a bad move and upset the board.

Perhaps she wasn't after Konoha's secrets. Perhaps the tense mood at the meeting itself had been her goal.

But Shikamaru's thoughts stopped here. He couldn't see her true intent for disrupting the peace between the five great nations. She was probably hiding something in Iwagakure. He couldn't make his next move until he saw what that was. If he sat here twiddling his thumbs, waiting for the next meeting, they would end up behind the behind the eight ball.

Defeat is not an option in this game. He'd had a bad feeling sitting heavy in his heart ever since the meeting.

"I assume that the Lord Hokage promptly rejected such a motion?" Ro asked, nostrils flaring, perhaps because he was indignant at the Tsuchikage's unreasonable demand.

"No."

"What reason did she give for her demand?"

"She brought up the scientific ninja tool Boruto used in the chunin exams and the subsequent attack by Otsutsuki. Plus, as a bonus, she even railed about Sasuke's work as a spy. She came in hard with this idea that Konoha was trying to pull away from the other countries. It was all Naruto could do to protest that she was wrong. And small wonder. Anyone'd be flustered after getting put through the wringer like that. The Tsuchikage wasn't interested in hearing what we had to say. She demanded we have an answer for her before the next meeting and stormed out. There wasn't much to be done after that."

"Not, like, much to be done with a woman like that," Hinoko spat.

Kurotsuchi was his comrade, someone he'd spent a lot of time in discussion with when he was younger. She was not a "woman like that"—intractable, fractious. He wanted to defend her on that point, but it seemed inappropriate when he was about to send these two Anbu into Iwagakure because of her.

"It makes no sense, Iwagakure saying all that. So I want you to look into it."

"Which is to say, you wish us to investigate the internal situation of Iwagakure?"

"Exactly. There has to be something." He was very nearly convinced of it.

"But…" Hinoko said in a clear voice and crossed her arms as she stared into space. Shikamaru turned his gaze on the talented ninja and waited for her to continue. "If it's like you say and something fishy's going on in Iwagakure, like, it might be difficult to get in. If the enemy's already on alert, security inside the village'll be tight."

"Which is exactly why I chose you two."

"Wha—?" Hinoko looked at Shikamaru, her face red.

"Who was it who snuck into the Land of Silence with you? I know better than anyone what kind of power you have."

"With such praise heaped upon us, you do make it impossible for us to refuse."

Ro could freely manipulate chakra. He could make his own chakra look like someone else's and even cloak the chakra of nearby comrades, an ability that had a wide range of applications. Using this jutsu, he should be able to easily slip past even the most vigilant of guards. Hinoko, meanwhile, was able to sever her targets' chakras with fine chakra needles she released from her fingertips. In other words, she was a brilliant assassin. If she temporarily cut off the chakra of any watchful eyes, she would make the target feel that they were carrying out their duties perfectly while she waltzed in right in front of them.

"Additionally, I'll enact one more plan."

"Any more reinforcement and, like, they'll just be in the way."

"I'll leave the actual work to you two," he said. "I'll be moving on my own."

"What?!" Hinoko shouted, caught off guard. She might have grown up now, but she had not outgrown her habit of crying out when faced with surprise.

After the dust settled in the Land of Silence, Shikamaru had invited Temari out on their first date. Hinoko had been standing off to one side, and the instant the question left Shikamaru's lips, the Anbu ninja shrieked with delight, sounding much more like an average girl her age than a hardened warrior. The cry had made a distinct impression on him. But he hadn't heard of this girlish side causing her to make any major blunders. She managed to draw an impressively sharp line between the two sides of herself when she was on duty.

"I'm going to Iwagakure, too," Shikamaru confirmed.

"Do you mean to say that you will be accompanying us?" Ro asked.

"No, I'm going to hold my head high and walk in through the front door. I haven't played shogi with old man Ohno-ki in a while, and I've already sent him a letter. If I just go ahead without waiting for his answer, he'll curse and call me names, but he'll let me in."

"I see." Ro nodded several times. "If Lord Shikamaru, Konoha's second-in-command, will be travelling that route, then the eyes of the guard will turn in his direction. We are to enter the village during this opening."

"That's exactly it."

"You don't have to, like, do that." Hinoko pursed her lips tightly. "We can do it just us, like."

"That's not it, Hinoko," Shikamaru replied. "I have something I want to confirm directly with the old man."

"I-I told you, like, don't call me Hinoko!"

"You just said so yourself, though."

"Shut up!"

"Will you just stop, Soku?!" Ro snapped. "Well, perhaps you could have some *kinoko* mushrooms and calm down?"

"Don't go dragging out the kinoko trying to get a play with Hinoko!" she yelled. "There are, like, limits. The quality of your jokes lately is, like, seriously going down, old man."

"Ngh!" Ro looked wounded.

It was precisely because the two of them could pierce the tension in a room like this that he could trust this difficult mission to them.

"All right. I'm counting on you both."

"Don't just, like, go getting the last word in there!" Hinoko nodded at Shikamaru, a wry smile coming across her face.

4

I can't just go wandering into another village…

Shikamaru keenly felt his own position all over again. He took his first days off in three months and headed toward the village of Iwagakure on his own. A group of ninja appeared at the village border to greet him. They presented themselves as guards, but he knew that they had been observing him for a while already.

He didn't want a meeting with Kurotsuchi. This was at

most a personal trip. Even after he told them quite plainly that he was there to visit Ohnoki, doubt remained in the eyes of the Iwagakure ninja. The nervous faces of the men guiding him through the village confirmed his suspicions that Kurotsuchi's behavior at the meeting had indeed been part of some deliberate plan.

Iwagakure was in crisis.

With no interruption from Kurotsuchi, Shikamaru obediently allowed himself to be led to Ohnoki's home. It was a small house; past the entryway, there was only a parlor and a bedroom. Ohnoki laughed that it was plenty for a single broken-down old man. Shikamaru felt like he was seeing a true ninja in the former Tsuchikage, his life modest, with no boasts of splendor after finishing out his service.

"That's check, old man," Shikamaru said to Ohnoki, the shogi board between them, his voice slightly louder than normal. Ohnoki was starting to lose his hearing, so he didn't always hear people speaking at a normal volume.

"Mm." Leaving his rook five squares ahead of the king, Ohnoki launched a general into Shikamaru's end. He was so focused on his attack that he didn't realize he was in check. He apparently hadn't heard Shikamaru.

"Hey, old man!" He tried shouting at Ohnoki, who had brought his face down to the board.

"What?" This shout reached Ohnoki, and he glared at Shikamaru with the sharp gaze that was very much the same as it had been when he was still called a legendary stone ninja.

"I said, that's check. If you keep going there…"

Ohnoki noticed the presence of the rook. "What am I doing?! Real blunder there. Take back."

"You said no take backs before."

"This here's just a simple oversight. You can go ahead and let me have it."

"I told you more than once that it was check." Shikamaru sighed. "You're the one who ignored me."

"Hwaa?!" With a deep furrow digging into his brow, Ohnoki flipped the shogi table from the bottom. He stood up and, after taking two or three wild breaths through his nose, he turned to Shikamaru and snapped out his index finger. "One more time!"

"You sure about that?" Shikamaru asked, scratching his head.

The old Iwagakure ninja squared his shoulders and nodded. "You can spend the night today, I s'pose. So then we have plenty of time still. I'll deign to play you."

"Whoa, whoa, you'll 'deign' to play me? That's my line."

"What did you say?!"

"Nothing."

The old man's blood surged when the contest grew heated, of course. His powerful anima radiated from his body, though much smaller now in his old age.

Happy to see the former Tsuchikage was still in good health, Shikamaru picked up the overturned shogi table and gathered up the pieces. "So, uh…"

"What?"

So the old man *could* hear him. It could be that his ears simply got better when he was on edge, but Shikamaru suspected the old man only pretended he couldn't hear when it was convenient for him. But then what about missing the check earlier? Shikamaru decided that if the old man were so inclined, voices would reach him. He might have been old, but he was still the former Tsuchikage.

He began to arrange the pieces on the table with quick smooth movements. Dropping his eyes to the game board, he asked, "What's going on in Iwagakure exactly?"

Ohnoki wavered. It wasn't agitation. He was suddenly tensing up. He must have known Shikamaru hadn't just come to play shogi.

So we come to the heart of the matter…

A heavy air rose up between them, like the presence of a third person watching the proceedings.

Shikamaru pressed on. "Did you know that your granddaughter demanded Konoha disclose confidential info at the last meeting?"

Ohnoki said nothing.

Shikamaru had already finished lining up the pieces. Even so, they only stared at the board. Neither moved to start a new battle.

"Kirigakure's Mizukage also acted like he was in agreement with Kurotsuchi even though Chojuro's always been friendly toward Konoha. Iwa and Kiri are both dependent on water and mineral resources. And it looks to me like there's some kind of connection there."

"I'm retired," Ohnoki muttered, his face stern, his eyes fixed downward. "I left village matters to my granddaughter."

Shikamaru drew the ashtray by his knee toward him and pulled a cigarette from his breast pocket. Staring at Ohnoki, he brought a flame to the end of it. He slowly inhaled and then exhaled hazy smoke before asking, "I seriously doubt a man like you's totally in the dark. Is there something happening in this village that you can tell a man from Konoha?"

"Why? Would you stop already?" Ohnoki picked up one of his pawns, and then said slowly, "The world might be at peace, but a ninja's a ninja."

Shikamaru heard the door open, followed by the sound of heels clacking across the floor. The sliding door separating the parlor from the entryway had been left open, and now a slender woman dressed in black appeared there.

"Kurotsuchi," Shikamaru said.

"Give us a heads-up if you're coming, Shikamaru. Your visit was so sudden, I couldn't give you a proper welcome." Kurotsuchi looked down on him coolly, hands on hips, pale leg peeking out from the slit in her skirt. The faint smile on her lips seemed particularly malicious.

"Got some time off for the first time in ages. And when I realized I hadn't played shogi with the old man lately, I couldn't just sit there, so I wandered over your way. My son plays nothing but video games. He never sits down to shogi with me. I've been dying for a partner lately."

"Oh dear. Really?" Not moving to take off her shoes, Kurotsuchi continued to look down on him. Ohnoki didn't so much as glance at his granddaughter. There seemed to be kind of friction Shikamaru couldn't read between the two of them.

It had been Ohnoki who trained his granddaughter, the possessor of a Kekkei Genkai, to be the Tsuchikage. It was no exaggeration to say that he had created the current Kurotsuchi. They had a powerful bond not just as grandfather and granddaughter, but as ninja as well.

What on earth happened then?

"Say, Shikamaru?" Kurotsuchi started.

"What?" Still seated, Shikamaru accepted the cruel gaze squarely as he crushed his cigarette out in the ashtray.

"What are you trying to get my predecessor to tell you?"

"What's that supposed to mean?"

"Don't play dumb," she snapped.

Ohnoki sat frozen between them, his eyes lowered.

"You came to dig into the matter of the other day, I assume?"

"If I was here on official business, I would have made a formal request as a ninja of Konoha," Shikamaru told her. "Don't misunderstand me here. I really did just come to play shogi with the old man."

"So then *I'll* ask *you*." Kurotsuchi spread her hands out. "Is Konoha going to accept my request? Or refuse it?"

Why are you in such a rush with this?

She was a woman with a good head on her shoulders. Normally, she would have said nothing about Shikamaru coming into Iwagakure by himself like this. She would have simply looked past it. And they were still very much in the early stages of the game. She had nothing to gain from pressing the issue now.

"We're still discussing it," he said.

"I would have assumed you were too important to take time off and dawdle here at such a critical time," Kurotsuchi spat, her voice dripping with irony.

"I just happened to have some days saved up."

"And this is how you chose to spend your precious time off?"

"There's no room for me in the house at home."

"Goodness, poor you."

"Let it go already."

"I can't simply leave my old comrade like this. How about I talk to Temari for you?"

"You'll only make things worse. Don't." He sighed. Not when they were in the middle of a fight over their anniversary.

"Oh my. Temari and I used to be good friends, you know."

"That's not the point. This is a family issue."

"Hmm. My condolences."

"Shut up."

As they parried and countered in this absurd and detached conversation, neither looked away from the other.

"Don't you think it would be best if you left?"

"Oh?" Shikamaru stood up. "Sorry, old man. I'll head out for today. Once things settle down, I'll come play again."

"I'll be waiting," Ohnoki said sadly, still staring at the board.

On the step up into the house, Shikamaru pulled his shoes

on. "Thanks for having me," he said over his shoulder.

"Take care on the way home." There was no malice in Kurotsuchi's voice.

As soon as he returned to Konoha, Shikamaru went back to work. He'd already had to squeeze his schedule and shoehorn in the time off to start with. He didn't have any extra for lazing around the village.

Konoha had also been busy while he was away. It wasn't as though his work would simply wait because he was not in the office. While he'd been in Iwagakure, three mountains of paper had arisen on the desk he'd so painstakingly cleared, so tall that they looked ready to topple over at any second. A mere three days away from this place, and this was what he came back to. What would happen if he got sick? The thought sent a chill up his spine.

We've got to rethink the approval process.

Too many things required a final stamp from Shikamaru. Once he had taken a look at the papers, he would pass about half of them on to Naruto. This was how daily business of the village was carried out, so he could only complain so much, but they had to make at least a few changes to the system. The burden on both himself and the Hokage was simply too great. At present, if something unforeseen happened to one or both of them, much of the village's business would grind to a halt. They needed to bring on capable staff to spread out the approvals beyond just two people.

He scanned one document after another. These papers,

dense with neat handwriting, were the crystallization of the earnest efforts put in by members of every department. It took him only a few seconds to scan each page and affix a stamp of either approval or rejection. He also made sure to remember everything he read so that he could point out contradictions or shortcomings if he were asked the reason for rejection later.

He was used to it. Every day, he was bombarded with paperwork, so his reading speed had increased. That was all there was to it.

I'm getting stronger at these sorts of acrobatics and nothing else.

Meanwhile, the techniques of a ninja's core foundation were limited to his self-complacency, no matter how much he trained. He'd stopped going on missions more than ten years ago already. There was no way of assessing the potency of his techniques since he never executed them in an actual battle anymore. For all he knew, his son could be sharper than he was nowadays.

No, no. I'm his father. I haven't lost to him yet. He didn't have much confidence in this assessment, though.

"This is from the water department," said a voice

"Just put it there," he replied without looking up. More than two hundred people came and went from his office every day. If he had a conversation with each and every one of them, that alone would take up all his time, so he generally kept things brief.

As he worked through the piles of documents, he thought about Iwagakure. Thanks to Kurotsuchi's well-timed interruption, he hadn't been able to get anything from Ohnoki. Fortunately, his visit had only been a diversion. The real point had been to sneak in the team of Ro and Soku. The fact that they still hadn't reported to him likely meant they'd been successful. Kurotsuchi was definitely hiding something. He was almost certain.

"Lord Shikamaru." A woman's voice came from the other side of the mountains of papers.

He pressed his seal onto a statement regarding the collection of garbage from the sanitation department. "What?" He did not look up.

"Do you have a minute?"

As he tossed the document into the "approved" tray, he looked between the mountains of papers to a young ninja with her hair pulled back in two bunches.

Kazamatsuri Moegi, the jonin who led Shikadai's team. Had something happened to his son?

He stopped his hand and leaned back in his chair for the first time in a few hours. "What's up?" He didn't mention his son. Moegi's team included not only Shikadai, but also Cho-Cho and Inojin. He didn't want to be one of those parents who got overprotective and overemotional about "my son, my son."

"It's about Shikadai."

He exhaled through his nose and looked straight up at her. "You're his instructor. Everything relating to Shikadai as a ninja is up to you. I've got no business telling you anything."

"I do appreciate you saying that. But would you perhaps allow me to discuss him a little with you today?"

I see. What could have happened that his father have to hear about?

Her round eyes shining with the strength of her will, Moegi began to speak. "Ever since the chunin exams, Shikadai and our team have been getting a lot of attention. We also have more B-rank missions now."

The chunin exam finals weren't solely for the purpose of recognizing when young ninja reached the rank of chunin, and the villagers of Konohagakure weren't the only ones who came to watch; there were also large crowds of ninja from other villages, not to mention the daimyo from the Land of Fire and VIPs from other countries who made their way to the site in order to select skilled work partners. The finals were a place for people inside and outside the village to directly assess the abilities of each ninja. Performing conspicuously well in the chunin exam finals was the shortest route to great success as a ninja.

Shikadai had cleverly snared Iwagakure's Gaara's treasured child Yodo with his strategy and secured the victory with his Shadow Paralysis jutsu. This appeared to have led to some praise. It was a fortunate outcome.

"An S-rank mission's come to us at the request of a client," Moegi told him.

"An S-rank? Out of the blue?"

Ninja missions were divided up into ranks of A, B, C, and D. The very highest rank was S. Normally, S-rank missions were assigned to jonin. Shikadai and his team hadn't even made it to chunin, so this was not the sort of mission they could accept. The fact that the client could make them take it at a mere "request" meant that whoever it was, they were a fairly big deal.

"Can they do it?"

"It *is* an S-rank," Moegi noted. "But they'd be bodyguards for the daimyo's family. It wouldn't be difficult."

"Traps come dressed in bodyguard clothing, sometimes. Best not let your guard down," he warned.

"I would never." Moegi wasn't the sort of ninja to talk about things like this for no reason. Something was off.

Shikamaru set a hand to the tip of his beard and asked, with hard eyes, "Did something happen?"

"Shikadai refused the mission."

"What?"

"No matter what I say, he holds firm. All he'll say is that it's 'a drag.' Cho-Cho and Inojin tried to talk to him too, but he won't listen."

His son wasn't the type to insist on things like that. Temari hated selfishness more than anything, so ever since he was little, Shikadai had gotten a serious earful whenever he insisted on his own ideas without thinking of other people. So why now?

"I thought perhaps you might know something, Lord Shikamaru." Moegi lowered her eyes apologetically.

What she was really asking was whether something had happened at home. The answer was no. Or was it? He *was* in the middle of a cold war with his wife. He'd said he would make up the anniversary to her, but he still hadn't done anything. Their conversations had devolved to the bare minimum. If Moegi was asking after changes in the family, that was definitely one.

Was Shikadai foolish enough to squander a chance like this over something like that? No. Definitely not. This was a normal fight between a married couple. Shikadai wasn't such a little kid that he'd be so shaken up over that.

"Nah, I haven't heard anything," he replied.

"You haven't?"

"What happened with the mission?"

"The client was apparently very insistent that it be our team," she said. "But the liaison department explained the situation to them and another team was dispatched."

That struck him, too. Why would they be so insistent on having Shikadai and his team do it?

"Would you ask Shikadai about it, Lord Shikamaru?"

"Okay." Shikamaru nodded. "Sorry for the trouble."

"Not at all." Moegi bowed deeply and left the room.

Shikamaru stood up and headed for the roof. He laid down there and lit a cigarette.

"Honestly. What exactly happened there?"

The strangeness in Iwagakure, the mountain of routine work, and now even his son...

The clouds drifting in the sky spun round and round.

I'm so busy, it's making me dizzy.

"That's exactly right," he muttered absently as he puffed on his cigarette.

It was nearly midnight by the time he was able to go home. Temari and Shikadai were both already asleep. He walked down the hallway quietly and slowly opened the sliding door to his son's room.

"Hey, Shikadai," he called out to the pile of blankets.

"What?" his son replied sleepily, back still turned to Shikamaru.

"I heard you turned down an S-rank mission?"

Silence.

"Why?"

Silence.

"You got some reason why you don't wanna answer?"

Silence.

"Hey, you listening to me?"

"I'm listening."

There was no strength in his voice. Maybe it was because he'd been asleep, or maybe he felt guilty. Shikamaru blamed all the time he spent at work away from his family for his inability to read his son's emotions, which seemed to grow more complicated with each passing day.

"So this mission, why—"

"'Cause it was a drag."

"What?"

"It was a drag, so I said no." His son's voice took on a sudden note of anger.

"What kind of reason—"

"Just let it go," Temari said abruptly, from behind him.

When he looked back over his shoulder, his wife had turned her gentle gaze on him. "Shikadai's got things going on, too. And he has an early mission tomorrow. Let him sleep."

He let out a deep sigh to calm himself. "G'night," he said to his son, whose back was still turned to him.

He got no reply.

6

Once every seven days, most of the village took a day off. At times when Shikadai and other ninja on the front lines did not have a mission assigned to them, they were ostensibly on standby and also had the day off. But Shikamaru had no holidays. Even when everyone else had the day off, he would go into the office to catch up on the work he'd fallen behind on during the rest of the week.

Still, on these holidays alone, he wouldn't go into the office until lunchtime. These mornings at home were Shikamaru's sole break.

He couldn't complain. Naruto lived on the same schedule as Shikamaru, while also dealing with additional cumbersome tasks, like meeting with VIPs from various countries—hence Naruto's regular use of Shadow Clones. With a wry smile, he had once told Shikamaru about the time his son had found out he was a Shadow Clone in the middle of an important family event.

Given the pace that the Hokage had to keep up, Shikamaru couldn't very well complain his own busyness. And he wanted to be do more for Naruto. This thought had been on Shikamaru's mind ever since he'd become the Hokage's advisor.

Shikamaru generally spent the fleeting moments between finishing breakfast and leaving the house on the veranda. And today once again, he enjoyed a brief respite, thinking about absolutely nothing at all while he looked out at the trees in the bright light of the morning sun.

"So about Shikadai."

Shikamaru turned his head to look into the living room. At some point, Temari had come to sit there. She stared into her tea with a strange look on her face. Shikamaru spun on his bottom to face her through the veranda door.

"And where is he?"

"He left early this morning. He said he was going to go hang out with Boruto and his friends."

Despite his duties as a ninja, Shikadai was still a child. He was of the age where if he had been a non-ninja child of the village, he would have been leading an easy life, playing with his friends every day.

"About that mission he refused."

So it is about that…

He sat up straighter and waited for Temari to continue.

Face still turned to her teacup, his wife raised her eyes to Shikamaru and began to speak slowly. "I guess what the client really wanted was to get closer to you. They were trying to build a relationship with you, the Hokage's advisor, so they requested Shikadai's team take the mission. And then Shikadai got wind of this, so…"

"What?"

Temari's words pierced his heart. He couldn't believe his own position would have an impact on Shikadai's work. He would be lying if he said the idea had never crossed his mind. but he sternly told the people of Konoha on a daily basis that they were not to give his son any special treatment. He hadn't even dreamed that someone from another village would use

Shikadai to get close to him.

"So then who's this client?" he asked.

Temari shook her head. "Shikadai doesn't know. He just said it's some VIP from some small country."

There were any number of smaller nations that would try to leverage the power of a large country like the Land of Fire. There was no doubt that this client had some kind of ulterior motive.

"Is that why he didn't tell me?" Without knowing it, he had hurt his son. Shikamaru may not have made a mistake himself, but his own existence had put an obstacle on Shikadai's ninja path. "Dammit."

"Don't blame him."

"I know," he said, his heart heavy.

Temari turned her eyes toward the garden. "A visitor."

He didn't need to turn around. The aura wafted through the hedge into the garden. This person clearly wanted him to notice her.

An orange chakra. Hinoko. She was back from Iwagakure.

"We'll pick this up again later," he said, standing.

Temari silently got to her feet and grabbed his jacket from where it hung on the wall. And then she went around behind her husband and helped him into it in a practiced movement.

"I'm off then."

"Mm-hmm." His wife's voice was much gentler now.

I really have to think of some way to make it up to her.

Shikamaru stepped over the threshold and out of the house.

The park on that holiday morning was full of children playing with their fathers. He could count on one hand the number of times he had played with Shikadai like that. It was always work, work, work.

Shikamaru's eyes were always turned outward. He never spared a glance for his family. And now he had hurt Shikadai as a result. He had no idea how he could make this up to him. He could say he was sorry that Shikadai had had to go through that because of him, but his son was clever enough to know only too well that Shikamaru hadn't actually done anything wrong. An empty apology would only further hurt his son. And in that case, it was better not to apologize at all. That said, he couldn't exactly just leave it, either.

"Family is such a drag." Shikamaru settled himself onto a bench beside Hinoko.

"I don't live with my parents, and, like, I don't have my own family yet, so I dunno," Hinoko replied curtly, her eyes turned toward the families at play. He hadn't felt like hearing her report in his office, so he'd selected a park near his house. The parents were totally absorbed in their children, and there was also a good bit of ambient noise, so he wasn't worried about being overheard.

"You should start your own family, Hinoko," he said. "You're old enough to be a mother already. Not that it wouldn't be a loss for Konoha if you stopped working."

"Like, what you just said is sexual harassment," she noted archly.

"It is?"

"It, like, is."

"Sorry 'bout that."

"You're not, like, actually sorry. I've told you a million times not to use my name. You, like, use it on purpose." Hinoko smiled.

Shikamaru smiled back.

"About Iwagakure," she said, her face tensing again.

Shikamaru listened as he watched a father and daughter

throwing a peach-colored ball back and forth.

"The Land of Earth's behind the way Kurotsuchi behaved at the last meeting of the Five Kages."

"The daimyo?"

Hinoko nodded.

It seemed that Shikamaru's hunch that something fishy going on had not been mistaken.

"There's this country right next to the Land of Earth called the Land of Flowers."

"That's the small nation that specializes in flowers, right? Just like the name suggests. I heard the daimyo's famous for being kind to his people. Also, it's a pretty nice place to live for a small country."

"The soil there is very rich," she said. "They can make flowers, like, their specialty because they have this soil that is great for growing things."

So what did the Land of Flowers have to do with Kurotsuchi's recent behavior?

"Meanwhile, the better part of the Land of Earth is, like, rocky and mountainous. It's hard to grow anything at all. They, like, put together stuff like potatoes that can grow in poor soil, and somehow manage to get food to their people. So, like, they buy most stuff from other countries, trading with the minerals they have a ton of."

"But that's how pretty much every country gets by," Shikamaru noted.

"But if, like, you had someone weaker right next to you, someone who had something you didn't, you'd want it, yeah?"

"No way." Shikamaru's eyes grew wide, and he stared at Hinoko.

Mouth pulled into a straight line, the young Anbu ninja simply nodded once. And then she got to the heart of the matter. "The Land of Earth's going to, like, attack the Land of Flowers. Of course, the military force to do this will be the Iwagakure ninja."

"So Kurotsuchi is trying to chisel a crack or two into the alliance of the Five Kages," he mused.

"The Land of Flowers has long had an alliance with the Land of Lightning," Hinoko continued. "I guess the Land of Flowers had, like, the kind of crop failure that happens once in a million years, and the Land of Lighting stepped in to help them out. They formed this close bond that's made, like, the relationship between the two countries unshakeable even now."

"If the Land of Earth attacks Flowers, the Land of Lightning... Which means the village of Kumogakure won't sit back quietly." Shikamaru's head was spinning. His mouth raced to keep up with his thoughts. "If the Land of Earth says they're invading Flowers, then Iwagakure has no choice but to obey. And the other Kages aren't going to sit back and keep quiet about Iwagakure going to war. Especially not Darui. He'll stand up to Kurotsuchi if hostilities do break out. If the foundation of the alliance of the Five Kages is solid, Kurotsuchi will be alone. That's why she picked Konoha to be her victim. She had clearly talked with Chojuro before the meeting. She wanted him to cooperate with Iwagakure. In which case she wouldn't be standing alone. If she could reel in Chojuro by censuring Konoha, she'd be able to count on Kumogakure once the invasion of the Land of Flowers became known. So Kurotsuchi was laying the groundwork then."

"That's, like, exactly it," Hinoko said.

Shikamaru stared at the peach-colored ball dancing in the air. Ohnoki's words came back to him. *The world might be at peace, but a ninja's a ninja.*

Had Ohnoki been trying to tell him something?

The heart of the ninja was in battle. It was indisputable that the large majority of jutsu were specialized fighting techniques that had been created for the purpose of confronting ninja of other lands. The fundamental core of this creature called *ninja* was the fight. Ninja couldn't live in a world of peace. Was that why Ohnoki had said that to him?

No. The old man had been a driving force behind the alliance of the five hidden villages. He was one of the heroes who had fought for peace even while his wounds in the last great war had brought him to the brink of death. Would a man like that talk about destroying the very thing he had worked so hard to build?

Plus, the matter at hand did not originate with Kurotsuchi herself. The daimyo of the Land of Earth wanted the Land of Flowers and its productive farmland—that was where this all started. Ninja and daimyo may have put on a front that they were working together, but policy in the hidden villages was controlled by the daimyo's authority. If the village of Iwagakure hoped for peace but the Land of Earth called for chaos, the ninja would have no choice but to obey.

That was what Ohnoki had been trying to tell Shikamaru. Thinking about it that way, it all made sense.

But was this system really acceptable? Should ninja always obey the daimyo? Could they cast aside even the peace cultivated through the sacrificed lives of so many of their brethren if the daimyo ordered it?

"I'm definitely not gonna let that happen," Shikamaru muttered, raising his thin eyebrows."I can't allow a great nation to steal the peace of a small country outright. We're gonna have to keep those kids from having their parents ripped away from them."

Hinoko nodded quietly beside him.

"Are Ro and the others still in Iwagakure?"

Shikamaru said.

"My team's, like, still there, too."

"Keep digging into the situation in Iwagakure. If you find anything, report to me right away. We'll manage something here on our end somehow."

"Like, roger." She rose.

"I'm counting on you."

Smiling slightly, Hinoko nodded.

Shikamaru looked up at her. "Forgive me for the sexual harassment?"

"I'm, like, filing a suit when I get back." She stuck her small tongue out at him and vanished.

"Okay then. Guess I should get going."

Reluctantly, Shikamaru stood hurried off to find his good friend, who was most likely in the Hokage's office. A job awaited them.

It was going to be a drag.

TACTICS

1

Naruto was speechless as he glared at the reports sitting on his desk. Hands still in his pockets, Shikamaru stared at his friend frozen before the papers he himself had written up.

"I-is the Land of Earth really..."

"This is reality right here. If you really think about it, it's way easier to deal with an outsider enemy. The shinobi from different villages can pull together to fight an enemy like that. But real war's not so simple as all that. Now the enemy are ninja just like us, from another village. Countries and villages have their own individual motives. The idea that all villages would cooperate is at best idealistic."

Naruto gritted his teeth. He might have been the purest person Shikamaru knew. Naruto believed utterly in people's ability to come together and understand one another. To his credit, Naruto's lofty goodwill had indeed changed a great many people. He had even bridged the gap with his good friend, who had stepped off the path and become a rogue ninja, and gotten him to choose the path of living as comrades once more. There was no way that *this* Naruto would be able to quietly accept what Shikamaru was saying.

But Shikamaru needed Naruto to understand reality. People couldn't live on ideals alone. Kurotsuchi and the Land of Earth had their own agendas.

"Why would they go invading another country *now*?" Naruto muttered. "If they're having a hard time, they could just discuss it with the other nations. And if the daimyo can't make something work, Kurotsuchi could talk to us at a meeting of the Five Kages. If they don't have any good land, a country that can get plenty of food could help them out. I mean, that's the whole point of the meetings. That's the point of the alliance!"

Shikamaru felt the same way. The power of the alliance of the hidden villages of the five great nations rippled out to all the midsized and small nations on the continent now. If the alliance raised its voice, the ninja of the smaller hidden villages wouldn't be able to ignore their call. The foundation was there to discuss and resolve any issue that arose.

And yet the Land of Earth had decided on an attack on the Land of Flowers and was trying to make the village of Iwagakure bend to its will. Human fragility and emotion were clearly intervening in a way that was unfathomable with logic alone.

"This is what old man Ohnoki said," Shikamaru started, and Naruto lifted his face. "He said the world might be at peace, but a ninja's a ninja."

"A ninja's a ninja…"

Shikamaru nodded silently.

If they just sat back and watched, the Land of Earth would

invade, and the calm and peaceful life of the Land of Flowers would be destroyed by the ninja of Iwagakure. In which case, the Land of Lightning would intervene, given its many years of alliance with the Land of Flowers. So naturally, Kumogakure would also get involved in the struggle. If Chojuro's Kirigakure ninja added their might to Iwagakure's, then the chaos would be further accelerated. And it wasn't as though Konohagakure and Sunagakure would stand by silently. They might all be dragged into a fight that could swallow the continent.

The Fifth Great Ninja War...

The unpleasant words flitted through his mind. If they were once again plunged into a great war, they wouldn't be able to bring it to an end the way they had the last time. There was no external enemy to unite them.

Everything would collapse. Led by the daimyo, the five great nations would withdraw into the shells of their own countries, and the ninja of the hidden villages would be forced onto a path of blood, mindlessly felling ninja from other villages. And this unproductive fighting would continue for all eternity.

"Shikamaru." The hero who had ended the great war looked up, his eyes full of sadness. "Whatever else we do, we have to stop this war. Our kids don't know real war. For them, this peaceful village is the world of the ninja. Old man Ohnoki's ninja and what Boruto and the kids think a ninja is are two fundamentally different things. I don't want those kids to have to go through everything we experienced."

The Hokage closed his eyes. What did he see on the backs of his eyelids now? Hyuga Neji? Uchiha Itachi? So many ninja had been lost in the fierce fighting.

The phantoms that rose up in the back of Shikamaru's own mind were his father and master. The unhealed wounds that he had sealed away deep in his heart throbbed. He pulled a cigarette from his pocket and put it in to his lips. There was no smoking in here, so he just held it in his mouth. He could feel his master close to him when he did. That man was always smoking. His shoulders were never tensed up around his ears. He'd given the grumbling Shikamaru the friendly push he needed.

"What should we do?" he asked Naruto, wedging the unlit cigarette between his index and middle fingers.

"We gotta stop Kurotsuchi no matter what." The Hokage's sky-blue eyes shone with the light of resolve.

When he held such clarity, Naruto was strong. And with his conviction he took off running. It was Shikamaru's job to forge a path for the Hokage to run on. Naruto had the absurd strength to charge down any road, no matter how rough. But even if he knew where he was going, he didn't necessarily know how to get there. It was up to Shikamaru to draw him a map.

"If we're going to stop Kurotsuchi, we're gonna have to meet her and talk."

"Yeah." Naruto nodded emphatically.

Shikamaru flicked the tip of his cigarette with his thumb as he spoke. "This invasion of the Land of Flowers was decided on by the Land of Earth. Kurotsuchi's not the mastermind here, it's the daimyo of the Land of Earth. She's just cooperating with him. So whatever we say to her, the invasion of the Land of Flowers is still going to go ahead unless we have a word with the Land of Earth's daimyo and get his head on straight."

"But if Kurotsuchi rethinks this, the Iwagakure ninja won't move," Naruto noted. "In that case, the Land of Earth won't be able to go ahead with the invasion."

"I highly doubt that Kurotsuchi has put so little thought into this that she would change her mind because you tell her to. She's got her own line of thinking here. You know as well as I do that she's not the kind of woman to blindly follow the daimyo's orders."

"Are you saying that Kurotsuchi wants war?!" Naruto stood up and slammed his hands down on the desk.

Shikamaru hadn't seen him this angry in a while. Maintaining his own composure, he said to his overexcited friend, "Not the strangest idea, is it? A ninja who wants to fight?"

"Ah!" Naruto cried out as though something had just occurred to him. Then he turned to Shikamaru with a curious expression.

"What is it?" Shikamaru asked.

"Maybe it's like Akatsuki or someone pulling strings behind the scenes. Like, they used a jutsu on Kurotsuchi and the daimyo of the Land of Earth."

Akatsuki was the group of rogue ninja that had triggered the previous great war. They had intended to collect the tailed beasts scattered throughout the five hidden villages and use the enormous amounts of chakra they possessed to cast a genjutsu on every person in the world.

"Naruto!" he said in a forceful tone, rebuking his friend, before calmly continuing, "Kurotsuchi's a talented ninja. She's not going to get caught up in a genjutsu as easily as all that. As for the daimyo, she would have checked into that herself. If someone was pulling the strings behind the scenes, she would have already taken care of them. It's easy to look for the enemy on the outside. It might be more comfortable to turn your eyes from reality like that. But you're the Hokage. This is a problem of country and country, village and village. Don't grab the easy lie of an external enemy to make yourself feel better. You have to face reality squarely and look for a way forward."

"Right... You're right. I know you're right." Lifting his face, Naruto nodded slightly.

"First—" Shikamaru started.

"A meeting of the Five Kages." Naruto continued. And then he laughed. He had changed since becoming Hokage. He didn't charge ahead on emotion alone the way he used to; he had learned how to figure out a way forward himself. Naruto had turned out to be a great Hokage.

Even so, there were still things only Shikamaru could do. Naruto was the shining sun of this village. Shadow always followed a powerful light. Shikamaru was that shadow, created by the Naruto's dazzling sun.

"At any rate, we say we want to talk about Kurotsuchi's motion from last time and meet again," he said, cigarette hanging from his mouth. "Then you cut right to the chase and ask her about the Land of Earth. It'll depend on how Kurotsuchi comes at you, but if we get it all out in the open, Darui and Chojuro will be forced to make a choice. It'd be bad if the meeting broke down there. We should probably talk to Gaara again beforehand."

"You mean get him on our side?" Naruto asked.

Shikamaru shook his head. "We're at best in a neutral position. We're not standing with Kurotsuchi or the Land of Flowers and Darui. We ask Gaara to be in the middle too. If Konoha and Suna can hold fast to the center, no one else will be able to make any careless moves."

"You take care of that then."

"I'm on it." And with that, Shikamaru had an enormous number of things to do: choosing a messenger to propose the meeting, deciding on a schedule, negotiating with Gaara. He probably wouldn't be able to return home for a while.

"Hey, Shikamaru!"

"Hm?"

"Put that cigarette out!" Naruto shouted. "I told you I'd get mad!"

Without realizing it, he had lit the cigarette. "Oh…" Shikamaru stared at the trail of smoke. "What a waste. Okay, leave the rest to me."

"You're going for a smoke?!"

Shikamaru ran out of the Hokage's office and raced up to the roof.

2

From the moment the Five Kages gathered, an oppressive air filled the venue—Kurotsuchi, her face grim; Darui, unhappy at having his everyday work interrupted by the urgent meeting; Chojuro, face tight in consideration of the argument that was about to happen; Gaara, taking his seat as calmly as ever, having been informed in advance by Naruto of the Land of Earth's reckless action; and in the center of them all was Naruto, looking intense, like he was about to go into the battle of a lifetime.

Naruto started them off. "Thanks for coming. I know you're all busy."

"So you're going to give us your answer then?" Kurotsuchi asked immediately, her voice inflectionless but exerting a tremendous pressure.

A faint smile on his lips, the Hokage looked at the black-haired Tsuchikage. "Actually, there's something I want to ask you today, Kurotsuchi."

"Goodness. And what's that?" Kurotsuchi replied, feigning innocence, while the corners of her mouth curled up.

Naruto put his hands on the table and leaned forward. "Is it true that the Land of Earth is planning to invade the Land of Flowers?"

"What?" Darui cried out, the color in his sleepy eyes changing. "Whoa, Naruto. What did you just say?"

"The Land of Earth is going to invade the Land of Flowers. That's what I said."

"What is the meaning of this, Kurotsuchi?!" Darui shouted.

Kurotsuchi furrowed her brow, seemingly annoyed, and shook her head from side to side with a sigh. Eyes still firmly trained on Naruto, she spoke slowly. "Konoha's always secretly digging up information on the other villages and trying to stand on top. While they scream in shrill voices about peace and bonds, in the shadows, they're using Sasuke and the Anbu and watching vigilantly for their chance to take control of the continent. The sooner the rest of you wake up to this, the better. None of us'll be laughing once they've got us pushed past the point of no return while we were lying around with our feet up."

"I'm telling you, Konoha would never do anything like that. Believe it."

"You can *say* whatever you want."

"Answer my question!" Darui interrupted. "Is it true the Land of Earth plans to invade the Land of Flowers?!"

"Yeah, it is." The Tsuchikaze shrugged.

Darui's cheeks tightened. "Kurotsuchi, what do you even know about the Land of Flowers?"

"They have a long-standing alliance with the Land of Lightning, right?" Kurotsuchi replied without looking at Darui.

"If you attack the Land of Flowers, the ninja of Kumogakure will absolutely come to their aid. And you know what that would mean, right?"

"When the Land of Earth moves, the ninja of the village of Iwagakure simply obey. Any enemies that stand in the way will be cleared away, a necessary sacrifice."

"Are you serious right now?"

"Stupid question." Kurotsuchi sidestepped Darui and looked to Naruto. "The disclosure of Konoha's secrets. What's your answer?"

"This is not the time for talking about that." Darui pressed.

Kurotsuchi finally looked at him. "Could you be quiet a sec? I'm talking to Naruto right now."

From where he stood behind Naruto, Shikamaru could almost hear the blood vessels in Darui's head rupturing.

The gentle Raikage was carried away by anger and leaped to his feet. "If you wish to fight me so badly, we can just do it right here and now."

Kurotsuchi lowered her eyes and sighed. "And what is you and I fighting here going to do? The Land of Earth's policy isn't going to change if I lose. Naturally, if you lose, I'm not going to start thinking differently all of a sudden. Either way, it's pointless."

"Just hang on a sec!" Naruto shouted. "What is this place even for then? This is supposed to be a time when the Five Kages come together and discuss things for the sake of peace, isn't it? Please, Darui. Sit down. Kurotsuchi, you too. Let's talk this out."

Still glaring at Kurotsuchi, Darui sat down, his body shaking. The black-clad Tsuchikage stayed where she was, however, and continued to press Naruto.

"Those of us who went through the great war know the power you and Sasuke wield. Konoha has two ninja with enough strength to wipe out an entire country. Do you really not understand what that means, Naruto?"

"Sasuke and I would never do anything to hurt anyone," Naruto protested. "We only use our power against groups like Akatsuki who want to tear down this peace. You gotta believe me."

"So Konoha intends to enforce order over the entire continent?" The Tsuchikage arched an eyebrow. "How is that different from controlling it, exactly?"

"That's not what we want!" Naruto roared, angry for once at a meeting. His face red, he said to Kurotsuchi, "We just wanna keep everyone safe. Trust me. Sasuke and I want peace more than anyone else."

"We'll protect the peace of our own village ourselves," she snapped. "No one asked you to step up and keep the whole world safe."

"Um?" Chojuro raised his hand. When Naruto nodded silently, the Mizukage pushed his glasses up. "Ninja work for their own countries. That's only natural. And indeed, it might be ideal for the Five Kages to join hands together like this. But if we stop fighting, ninja will no longer be ninja."

Shikamaru didn't miss the hint of pain bleeding into Chojuro's eyes. The Mizukage was fighting his own true self for the sake of his village.

"Perhaps it's about time we stopped pretending to play nice?" Chojuro said.

The air in the room froze. Everyone gathered there held their breath, picturing in the backs of their minds a future in which the solidarity of the five hidden villages had broken down.

Now...

While the meeting members were held fast by Chojuro's words, Shikamaru wove a sign and released his chakra.

"Wha—" The first to cry out was the one closest to him, Naruto.

The entire venue was enveloped in Shikamaru's shadow. The Five Kages, as well as the people who followed them, were unable to move so much as a finger.

Shadow Possession jutsu. The first time he'd used it in a conflict in a long time.

With the sign still held in front of his chin, Shikamaru glared at the Five Kages as he began to speak. "You've all been yammering on without a thought, but haven't you forgotten the key element here?"

"Stop, Shikamaru," the Hokage said.

Ignoring his friend, Shikamaru said to his foolish brethren, "It's true that Naruto and Sasuke have the power to destroy a country. But they're not the only ninja in Konoha. Even without them, the difference in strength between Konoha and the other villages is overwhelming. And if the head of Konoha, the Hokage, is willing to lay his life on the line to protect this alliance, then we ninja of Konoha will follow him, even if it means giving up our own lives. We won't allow anyone to disrupt this peace. Got it, Kurotsuchi? Chojuro? Listen good. If you say you're going to leave, then my shadow will crush your heads."

His jutsu was perfectly deployed. Kurotsuchi might have had a Kekkei Genkai, but it would be hard even for her to undo a shadow possession this perfect. If anyone would be able to, it would have been Naruto, who had full control over the power of a tailed beast.

"Kurotsuchi, Chojuro, do you really intend to go to war with Konoha?"

"Stop this mischief, Shikamaru," Gaara said in an even tone.

Out of the corner of his eye, Shikamaru looked into his brother-in-law's eyes beneath his forehead where the character for "love" was carved. "I'm serious."

"All the more so, in that case. There's no point in killing Kurotsuchi and Chojuro here. You know that better than anyone."

"There is a point. If word gets out that Shikamaru of Konoha disposed of the Tsuchikage and the Mizukage, ninja all over the continent will freeze in place. Everyone will know just how serious Konoha is. And if someone comes at us with their sword drawn anyway, we'll take them on when that time comes. Now, how about it, Kurotsuchi, Chojuro? There's one answer here. Yes or no. Tell me now."

"Ngh!" A groan slipped out from between Kurotsuchi's gritted pearly teeth. An inky black snake twined itself around the Tsuchikage's pale, slender neck. Her eyes glittered dangerously. "Do you understand what you're doing?"

Chakra gushed from the entire body of the Tsuchikage. Things were getting dicey.

Hurry and do it, Naruto.

"Stop!" Naruto shouted, sounding angrier than he had all day.

The Hokage's back burned a golden color. Shikamaru turned his head to look at him. The flames of battle burned in Naruto's eyes. The shadow that covered the room turned into black glass and shattered.

"Stop it! Shikamaru!"

A fierce blow made contact with his cheek, and Shikamaru fell to the floor.

"What are you even doing?! What is crushing us going to accomplish?!" Naruto yanked him up by his collar.

Shikamaru, motionless, said nothing. He averted his eyes. Naruto tossed him aside before bowing his head so deeply toward the other Kages that he almost scraped it on the ground.

"Sorry! He's not the kind of guy to do a thing like that! I'll really let him have it later! Forgive him!"

Kurotsuchi stood up. "So this is how Konoha does things."

"No!" Naruto protested. "As long as I'm around, I won't let anything upset our peace! Nothing! So please. Talk to the daimyo of the Land of Earth one more time about the Land of Flowers, Kurotsuchi. I'll give some serious thought to Konoha's secrets. I want to come up with something you can be happy with. We can't have another war ever again!"

"I believe you. But I don't know about the next Hokage. Someday, Konoha is going to be a threat to us," Kurotsuchi said, then left. Chojuro followed her out of the room.

"When Iwagakure moves, we will, too," Darui told Naruto, who still had his head bowed, before he too stepped out of the room.

"It's not as though the war has started yet," Gaara said, his voice tinged with warmth, and then he also departed with Kankuro.

On the way back to Konoha, Naruto was silent. Shikamaru also said nothing as he hurried, indifferent, along the road home.

When they were almost at the A-un main gates, Naruto said, back still turned, "Why would you do a thing like that?"

Shikamaru gave him the answer he had prepared. "I knew you would never allow it. You would definitely break my jutsu, and so win everyone over."

Naruto stopped and turned around. "It was your plan all along…"

"Now they've all accepted the threat of Konoha as a reality. We needed to make them understand."

"You… You just…"

"The gambit wouldn't have worked without both the might of Konoha and your passion as Hokage. It's just like Gaara said—the war hasn't started yet. We can't make any mistakes in this game, and it's far from over."

His friend nodded, a wry smile rising up on his face, and Shikamaru smiled in return before setting out again toward the village where his family was waiting.

3

For a few days after the meeting, Shikamaru's workload doubled. Then the onslaught suddenly evaporated. One day, he was working until late into the night, and the next he was free by evening.

Normally, he would use his free time to train in the deserted mountains or go home and relax, but today, his feet naturally turned toward the town. His destination was obvious. And he had no need of a map. He'd been to this particular place many, many times.

When he turned onto the road leading to the shop at the end of his journey, he spotted his old comrade watering the flowers. The countless bouquets in cylindrical silver containers could not be contained by the store itself, and they spilled out to line the street outside. The woman giving careful attention to each and every one of them was a florist through and through, but she had been a capable ninja once, and had come through any number of bloody battles with Shikamaru. Even now, she went on missions from time to time, flower in one hand, sword in the other.

"Well!" the woman said, and stopped her watering.

"Been a while, huh, Ino?" Shikamaru called out.

Yamanaka Ino had fought with Shikamaru during the great war as part of the Ino-Shika-Cho trio. Among the young ninja who hadn't experienced the war, the trio of Shikamaru's generation was still a topic of conversation even now. Individually their skills were a step behind the likes of Naruto and Sasuke, but as a three-person cell, a fundamental ninja formation, Ino-Shika-Cho were lionized as a head above the other ninja of the village. Some of the books written after the war even offered analyses of the trio's fighting techniques.

Ino had gotten married and carried out her duties as a ninja while tending to her family's flower shop. Her son Inojin, also a ninja, belonged to the same team as Shikadai. Shikamaru thought it was very like her to give everything she had to both her household and her work, always pushing forward undaunted.

He slowly walked over to stand in front of the shop.

"What's up?" Ino asked, still holding her hose. "Pretty unusual for you to come all the way to the store."

"Oh, uh, the thing is..." Shikamaru looked up and away as he scratched the back of his head.

"Uh-huh." Ino peered at him, a mischievous smile on her face. "So you're trying to make up for your anniversary then?"

Shikamaru was dumbstruck, and Ino laughed out loud.

"I didn't use my jutsu or anything, you know." Ino could use her Mind Transfer jutsu to enter the mind of another person.

"She told you?" Shikamaru asked, the corners of his mouth turning up, and Ino nodded. Because their sons were on the same team, Temari and Ino were known to chat with each other. They were both taking care of their families too, so they shared things in common.

"You went and forgot your anniversary." She sighed and shook her head. "You're the worst, you know?"

"Does Sai get that kind of stuff right?"

Ino's husband Sai used to be Naruto's comrade. He was not very good at openly expressing emotion, but he was a skilled ninja who'd trained with the Anbu since he was very small.

"He's a serious guy. He always makes sure to do something—for my birthday, our son's, Christmas. And of course, our wedding anniversary. If he's out of the village on a mission, he asks a colleague to give us presents."

Faced with this, Shikamaru couldn't very well argue his own case.

One little mistake and this is what I have to deal with?

The words "what a drag" spun round and round in his mind.

"So you came to buy some flowers then."

He had known Ino since childhood. And for generations, the Naras and Yamanakas had held each other in mutual respect as families that formed the Ino-Shika-Cho trio. He might have been the Hokage's advisor now, but to Ino he was still the same old Shikamaru who thought everything was a huge hassle. All he could do was nod obediently.

"In that case, you want this." Ino pulled out a single yellow flower from a silver canister standing against the wall of the shop. There were no leaves on the long, slender green stalk. Yellow petals spread out in all directions.

"It's a flower from Iwagakure," she told him. "Perfect for Temari, right?"

The yellow flower blooming at the top of the perfectly straight stalk did indeed make him think of Temari. This was actually the flower that Shikamaru had come to buy. If he were going to give Temari flowers, he figured it had to be these.

"Guess so," he agreed amicably, and Ino nodded, satisfied.

"You are, of course, going to make a bouquet, right?"

"Give me all the ones there—no, everything you've got," he said.

"Oh!"

Suddenly, he heard a familiar voice from the street. Turning to look, he found a figure so enormous it blocked the road.

"Choji," Ino greeted him, still holding the yellow flower.

Akimichi Choji, the third member of Ino-Shika-Cho.

A girl with a similar physique was standing next to him. Unlike the easygoing Choji, her lips were pinched shut, and she wore a complicated expression. Her skin was tan, a popular look with young girls. This was Choji's daughter, Cho-Cho. She was also on Shikadai's team. The Ino-Shika-Cho trio now belonged their children's generation.

"What's up?" Shikamaru asked. "You buying a flower for your daughter?"

"I prefer dumplings to flowers," Cho-Cho said before Choji could respond.

Choji smiled at her. "I have today off, so I figured we'd all go to Q, the whole family."

Yakiniku Q...

Choji was a regular at the yakiniku grilled-meat restaurant. Back when the three of them had been on the same team, they'd hung out at the restaurant too many times to count. This was the place they went to celebrate after the end of a mission when their instructor Sarutobi Asuma was still alive. Asuma's treat, naturally. The restaurant was permanently burned into the back of his mind.

"Cho-Cho," Shikamaru said. She raised her thin eyebrows slightly and cocked her head to one side. "Sorry about Shikadai."

"Why?" she asked.

"Oh, he turned down that mission, right?" Shikamaru said. "Just when you finally get an S-rank mission. Sorry about that."

"Whatever," Cho-Cho replied coolly.

That was all he got from her. She kept things simple. Shikamaru wondered if all the kids were like this these days.

"It's been a while since we've seen each other, so Daddy's gonna talk to these two for a minute," Choji said to Cho-Cho. "You go on ahead. I think Mom's already there."

"Got it." Cho-Cho trotted off without looking at her father.

"She looks more and more like you every day, huh?" Ino said to Choji as she watched her go.

"You think?" Choji rubbed his large belly happily.

Smiling wryly, Shikamaru lowered his face. "I have to apologize to you guys, too."

"What for?"

"About what?"

"Your kids had some trouble because of Shikadai. Sorry," Shikamaru replied, still staring at his feet. A child's misconduct was the parent's responsibility, but his blame ran deeper than that. If Shikamaru hadn't held the position he did, Shikadai would never have been put in that situation in the first place. He was responsible for this not just as a parent, but as a ninja.

Both Choji and Ino burst out laughing.

He hadn't been expecting this reaction. He lifted his face to find them smiling at him.

"Just when I was wondering what you were going to come out with, it's *that*?" Ino said, placing the hand gripping the hose on her hip.

"Shikadai's not the first member of the Nara family who hates a hassle," Choji noted. "We can just look straight to you if we're wondering about the source."

"That's why I'm apologizing…"

They laughed again loudly, as if rejecting Shikamaru's words.

"Shikadai for sure has his own way of thinking about all that," Choji said. His high-pitched voice didn't go with his fat body. "He's not the sort of kid who'd dump something just because it's a drag. The fact that you're apologizing to us is proof of that. Or am I wrong?"

"Don't you have something more important to do than apologize to us?" Ino asked.

Shikamaru raised a questioning eyebrow.

The kindhearted mother sighed. "Did you actually *talk* with Shikadai?"

"No..."

"You know, you're a genius at work, but when it comes to family, you're a total disaster," she told him.

He couldn't say a word to that.

"There's the thing with Temari, too," she continued. "You gotta really *see* your family. They're the ones supporting you behind the scenes so you can go out and do your job. A guy who can't take care of the people closest to him isn't going to be able to keep the village safe now, is he?"

Ino was right. He knew it. He'd thought about it. What he didn't know was how to communicate his thoughts and what he was feeling. And he closer a person was to him, the harder it was for him to open up to them in a real way. It was utterly pathetic.

"The two of you have opened my eyes. Thanks."

How could a man who can't face his family protect the village? Or avoid a war?

I have to get even stronger...

"Let's have dinner sometime soon." He turned his back to them and started walking. Ino was shouting something, but in his head, he was too busy interrogating himself to hear her.

"Ah!" Once he was pretty far from the store, Shikamaru remembered at last and came to a stop. "I forgot the flowers."

He really was the worst.

4

He continued to spend his days cramming into his head the contents of the papers he approved while thinking about the matter with the Land of Earth. Both tasks were important, and neither had room for errors. He no longer heard the voices of his staff when he fell into this meditative state of concentration. Over the last few days, it had become a matter of course that he only noticed a person after they had called his name loudly several times.

At the last meeting of the Five Kages, he had seeded the threat of Konoha in the minds of the other Kages, which was good, but now he was at a dead end. He'd told Naruto that they had to take the initiative, but he still had no concrete plan. Currently, his only option was to sit like a passive observer and watch for Iwagakure's next move.

He heard from Ro and Soku on a regular basis. Apparently, Iwagakure had begun to accept fewer missions. Shikamaru assumed they most likely intended to keep as many ninja as possible on standby in the village so that they'd be ready to mobilize whenever the order came in from the Land of Earth. He couldn't simply sit back and wait for the day of destruction. He *could* see a way forward, but the details were hazy.

This nut wouldn't crack if they only had ninja talking to each other. At the end of the day, the ninja bowed to the plans of the daimyo of the five great nations. Shikamaru could forsee a situation like the one developing because a daimyo's greed would disrupt the delicate balance of power.

He needed a radical plan to break this stalemate. For ninja, battle may be their core nature, but he sought coexistence among them, a peaceful world without fighting. Perhaps it wouldn't be such a bad thing for the ninja to disappear as the world moved toward peace. Some might have laughed this away as an immature fantasy, but Shikamaru was looking for eternal peace. A tragedy like the last great war must never be allowed happen ever again.

If there was no more war, then there would be no more need for the ninja. But the ninja jutsu and chakra systems were beneficial to society at large. If non-ninja could wield them effectively, then they would be even more useful. But that transfer of knowledge could only ever begin once there was an unshakeable peace. If ninja techniques were used for evil, their power could destroy the world, something that had been made amply clear to all in the last great war. Which was exactly why ninja techniques should only be shared when people had abandoned the path of hatred.

The road to achievingthis ideal world was still very rocky, but Shikamaru would never give up. He believed the day would come. Otherwise, there would have been no meaning in sacrificing time with his family to his work like this.

"…ru." From far off in the distance, someone was calling him.

A woman.

The thought passed through his mind as his hand calmly pressed his stamp down.

"…kamaru."

Too loud.

"Shikamaru!"

An angry roar was loud enough to scatter his thoughts. He jerked his head up to find a familiar face before him. Leaning forward, hand deftly placed between two mountains of paper, was the daughter of his former master.

"What? Mirai?"

"Don't 'what' me! Do you know how long I've been calling your name?" Scowling at Shikamaru's stunned response,

Sarutobi Mirai, child of Sarutobi Asuma, took her hand off the desk and put it on her hip. "You should really do something about that habit of not noticing what's going on around you."

"I'm thinking about serious business here," he told her. "I don't have time for trivialities."

"And what are you planning to do if someone comes along with their own serious business?"

"They'll just yell at me like you did."

"True…"

He could tell by looking at her tense face that Mirai had brought some new trouble for him.

Long, long ago, this girl would lisp "Shika!" and would throw herself into his arms whenever she saw. She was the only girl he'd raised as master and teacher. He made sure he kept his promise to his own master in heaven to protect when Mirai.. Even with the endless work he was doing to assist Naruto, he'd found the time to teach Mirai the fundamentals of ninjutsu once she started at the academy. Her father, Asuma, was the son of the third Hokage, so Mirai had the blood of a Hokage running through her veins. Her innate ninja abilities were so great that he sometimes thought it presumptuous to say he had taught her anything. After showing her something once, she picked it up immediately; by their next meeting, she would have thoroughly mastered the technique. He often thought that she didn't really need him.

But Mirai continued to call Shikamaru *master* and adored him to this day. While it flattered him when she would tell him without hesitation that he'd turned her into a real ninja, it was also embarrassing.

He laid his square seal down on the desk, settled back in his chair, and asked his loyal student, "So what fresh annoyance are you bringing to me today?"

"You know what's happening in this village in three days, right?" she asked.

"Don't answer a question with a question," he said, a smile spreading across his face, and then answered her. "The daimyo of the Land of Fire is coming to the village to meet with Naruto."

It was a good opportunity. They weren't going to get any further if they kept this conversation to the ninja alone. A meeting of the daimyo would open up a new front on the game and put a direct stop to the daimyo of the Land of Earth. This was Shikamaru's secret strategy to break open this stalemate he faced.

In his wildest dreams, he couldn't have planned for a better opportunity for Madoka Ikkyu, Land of Fire's daimyo, to visit Konohagakure. Through Naruto, he would get Ikkyu to convene a meeting of the five great nations. If they could make such a summit happen, the likes of which had only been done a handful of times in the long history of the continent, the game would advance to a new level. They had to persuade Ikkyu to call together the other daimyo, whatever it took.

"Did something happen with that?" Shikamaru asked.

"There's no issue with the meeting itself," Mirai replied. "But Lord Ikkyu will be accompanied by his son Lord Tento."

"You're not here to tell me what a chore babysitting is, are you?" He did not need her bringing every little thing like this to him.

"I wish that it were as simple as that." Her face clouded over.

"What's the matter?"

"Apparently, Mujina have their sights set on Lord Tento," she told him.

Mujina was a group of bandits. Their boss, Shojoji, a ninja who used a jutsu called Corpse Doppelganger, was classified as one of the bigger targets in the Bingo Book.

"So then the report of Mujina showing up in the village would be in this mountain somewhere." Shikamaru dug through the reams of paper on his desk and neatly pulled a single sheet out from near the bottom of a precarious pile. "Got it. Right. Boruto's team was given the mission of arresting them, right?"

"Yes." Mirai nodded.

"You still don't look happy."

"Most likely, causing a commotion in the village is just the tip of the iceberg for Mujina. They're really after Lord Tento."

"So they want us to take the bait and drop Mujina from our line of investigation?"

"I doubt Shojoji would even show himself to Boruto's team," she agreed.

Mujina abducts Tento… Force the enemy to take a pawn and then take the king. Maybe we can use Mujina.

"Watch Tento while he's in the village," Shikamaru instructed. "Don't take your eyes off him for even a second. When Mujina starts to move, let the abduction happen."

"What?" Mirai cried.

"Just hear me out." A hazy bloodlust shone in his eyes. "We let them abduct him, and then we quickly move in to rescue him. Okay? Listen closely. You have to let him be abducted."

"Why would we…"

She had brought this to him to prevent it from happening. Shikamaru gave her this order in full awareness of that fact.

"We're going to make Madoka Ikkyu owe us one."

Mirai was at a loss for words.

Regardless, Shikamaru continued. "You're up against Shojoji here. Don't let your guard down. Wipe them out after they abduct Tento and take him back to their hideout. You have to rescue Tento unharmed. And…" He took a deep breath. "Don't tell Naruto."

"What?!"

"If Naruto knows anything about this, he'll set a guard for Tento and prevent the abduction. Then it will all be meaningless. Tento gets abducted, and the ninja of Konoha save him. We need this to happen."

"What exactly are you thinking, Shikamaru?" She raised a curious eyebrow at him.

"Trust me, Mirai. This isn't just for the sake of this village. The future of the world's at stake."

He was trying to prevent a war. He couldn't bother with appearances. He'd been ready to stain his hands with darkness from the moment he decided to be Naruto's advisor. He by himself was more than enough to handle the dirty work.

"I'll leave the team makeup up to you. At any rate, don't take your eyes off of Tento. Got it?"

"Yes." Mirai left the room, looking troubled.

Three days later, Madoka Ikkyu and his son Tento arrived in the village of Konohagakure. At the same time, a report arrived from Boruto's team that three members of the Mujina bandits had been secured. Shikamaru was in the Hokage's office when Mirai brought word of the success of Boruto's mission to the Hokage.

"Boruto and his team, huh? Nice work!" Naruto put his hands on his desk and pushed himself up to his feet in delight.

"Hmm. Looks like they can get the job done." Shikamaru took a cigarette out of his pocket and put it in his mouth. "Mirai, you got a light?"

Mirai stared at him dumbfounded before answering coolly. "There's no smoking in here, Shikamaru."

"I know."

He stared into her eyes. There was a flicker of resolve in the double rings of her irises. *I am carrying out the mission you entrusted me with.*

Nodding slightly, he said, "Anyway, you said three members, yeah? Shojoji was a no-show?"

"*Corpse Doppelganger* Shojoji?" Naruto muttered, glaring into empty space.

"Yeah," Shikamaru said. "A big target in the Bingo Book. He copies the look and voice and even the memories of a person he kills and transforms into them."

"We gotta do something about him fast."

His friend's voice was stern, and Shikamaru felt reassured that he'd make the right choice in keeping this mission quiet. If Naruto knew about the Tento abduction, he'd prevent the incident before it happened. He needed to stop Naruto from looking too closely at Mujina, though.

"Well, leave Mujina to me," Shikamaru said. "You should focus on today's big meeting." Naruto's attention was diverted from further thought of Mujina when the "meeting" was mentioned. And Shikamaru was consumed with guilt for distracting Naruto from his concealed plan.

And then something surprising happened. After Tento was taken hostage by Mujina, he was rescued by Boruto and his team. Boruto had been assigned to watch out for Tento while he was in the village, and the two boys ended up becoming close. They'd opened up to each other in a real way and promised to be friends. Mirai reported all this in detail.

Once he learned that Tento had been abducted, as if the kidnappers had simply been waiting for the moment when his bodyguard duties ended, Boruto snuck into the Mujina hideout alone. Halfway through the fight, his team members arrived to help, and together, they got Tento safely back home. On top of that, they managed to capture the Mujina leader, Shojoji. The squad Mirai put together hadn't had to lift a finger.

"You don't know what would have happened if it hadn't been Boruto who came along. You did good. Anyway, it's not quite how I planned it, but the fact remains that Konoha ninja saved Tento."

"I'm sorry." Mirai bowed her head.

"You've got nothing to be sorry for. This works just as well. Don't worry about it."

"Okay." She paused. "Shikamaru?"

"What?" An unlit cigarette hung from his lips.

"What are you trying to accomplish here?"

He spun around on his chair. And then when he turned to face Mirai once again, the sparkle that lit up his eyes when he was on the frontlines had come to life once more.

"I am going to set up a game we can't lose."

5

"Talk to Ikkyu one more time," Shikamaru said to Naruto, who was sitting in the Hokage's chair.

"What's this about? I just talked to him, didn't I?" His blue eyes wide open, Naruto had a strange look on his face. He sighed as he leaned forward and put his elbows on the desk. "You've been weird lately."

"You can think I'm as weird as you want. Just get in touch with Ikkyu right away."

"And what exactly am I supposed to talk to him about?"

"About the Land of Earth." Shikamaru glared at him, a fight in his eyes.

Naruto took this in calmly. "We talked that out at the meeting the other day," he said slowly. "I got a firm promise from Lord Ikkyu that he would start working on the Land of Earth. There's no need to go to the Land of Fire and meet with him again."

"The situation's different now," Shikamaru insisted.

"You mean because of the abduction?" His blond eyebrows raised, and the Hokage's previously kind eyes took on a hard edge. "Shikamaru, you knew Lord Tento'd be abducted, didn't you? You deliberately let Shojoji and them flop around so they would take Lord Tento and then you could save him."

It was in the past now. It would have been a hassle if Naruto had known beforehand, but him knowing now couldn't change anything. Shikamaru nodded calmly. "I was the one who gave the order to say nothing to you."

"So you could make Lord Ikkyu owe us one, I guess?" As Hokage, Naruto had also learned to consider tactics of manipulation like this. But he never wanted to resort to these darker methods for leverage. That was fine. Shikamaru didn't want him to either. Naruto had to remain the light. He would take on the shadows himself.

Giving a deliberate snort of laughter, Shikamaru shrugged. "If you understand that, then you can figure out the point of meeting again yourself."

"That's not what I'm talking about," Naruto protested. "I'm saying you've been weird lately! Using your Shadow Possession to threaten the Five Kages, overseeing the abduction of Lord Tento…"

"I didn't oversee it," he replied. "I was monitoring it very closely. Even if Boruto's team hadn't rescued him, Tento would have been returned to Ikkyu without a scratch."

"And what did you plan to do if the worst happened and Lord Tento was killed?!" the Hokage snapped. "Were you going to take responsibility for that? I can't just let this go. I mean, using a child as a hostage for negotiation?"

"I've always known that you hate this sort of thing. That's why I did it, isn't it?"

"Shikamaru!" Naruto stood up, walked around his desk, and grabbed his friend by the collar. "You always keep every little thing to yourself. You have to trust me more."

Shikamaru didn't flinch at the sudden rough handling. "It's precisely because you're the Hokage that I can do this sort of thing. I was able to do what I needed to do at the meeting of the Five Kages and with Tento because I have faith in you."

"So what's so important that you'd get Lord Ikkyu in our debt?"

"A meeting of the daimyo of the five great nations."

"You..." Naruto released Shikamaru's collar.

"We're not going to get anywhere at this point with ninja talking to ninja," he said coolly, rubbing his neck. "We're at a standstill now unless the daimyo get together and talk this out."

Sighing, Naruto closed his eyes and shook his head. "I'm racking my brains here, too, okay? Even I know that we won't get anywhere like this. We can't have war ever again. But I can't see a way forward, however much we might want to make a move here. I thought about going to Iwagakure and talking with Kurotsuchi one-on-one, but I don't know if that'd do anything to improve the situation."

"That's not like you."

Naruto looked at Shikamaru with wide eyes.

"Think it and do it," he said to his sworn friend of so many years, smiling faintly. "That used to be who you were. If you had time to worry, you'd rather get moving. You've always forged your path forward like that."

"I guess so," Naruto said sadly, staring at his open hands.

"When you grow up, though, you have so much more responsibility. A whole lot of hassle. It weighs you down. Believe it. Responsibility hangs so heavy on your neck, you can't take a single step. And then you just get stuck in this thought loop, like maybe you should have done it the other way. Or like, no, *this* is the right way. It just never stops."

Naruto wasn't usually one to complain. As Hokage, he stood out front to lead the village of Konohagakure with an unflaggingly positive attitude. But he struggled. He worried and got weighed down. The burden he bore was greater than anyone in the village; he was responsible for so much, he couldn't exactly go running off however he pleased.

Naruto only spoke of these anxieties to Shikamaru, and then only occasionally. Shikamaru was the only one who knew this vulnerable side of Naruto.

"You wanna go up to the roof for a sec?"

"Smoke?" Naruto raised an eyebrow.

Shikamaru grinned and nodded.

"Fine. If you have to." Naruto followed him out of the office.

When they came out onto the roof, Shikamaru pulled out a cigarette and lit it. He let the smoke roll into his lungs before gently exhaling. The wispy trails of gray melted into the dazzling blue sky.

As he looked up at the clouds drifting from west to east, Shikamaru turned to his close friend. "Growing up, having a family, it's all a huge struggle. Sometimes, I want to just throw it all away and be by myself."

"I've never been happier than I am now," Naruto replied.

"You only say role model stuff now." Shikamaru sighed. "You used to be more honest with yourself, you know."

"Maybe."

They laughed, and then Shikamaru took a drag on the cigarette, which was now half ash.

"For all that I'm weighed down now, thinking about all these exhausting and annoying hassles, I'm way better at strategizing than I used to be. I think up new tactics and plans that would never have occurred to me before. It's not like I get scared and freeze up. I've lived more life so now I can see and play the best moves."

"When you talk so confidently, I can almost believe you're right about anything," Naruto remarked.

"At the very least, I *think* I'm right." He crushed the cigarette and dropped it into the circular ashtray. Even after he was done smoking, however, neither man moved to leave the roof.

"Hey, Naruto," he said. "I'm absolutely not giving up. We have to avoid a war above all else."

"I'm right here with you on that." The Hokage nodded.

"It's a delicate road, like walking across thin ice. We can't worry about how things look. And some of this stuff is bound to mess us up. You might have to play a couple cards you hate. Even so, you have to trust me. I'm not giving up on peace, right up until the bitter end. I don't want Boruto and Shikadai to have to go through the stuff of Asuma and Neji's time."

"Got it."

Shikamaru felt a warm hand on his back.

"I trust you."

"You turned out to be a real Hokage," Shikamaru said and put another cigarette in his mouth. He quickly lit it and exhaled smoke.

"You're smoking more." Naruto pursed his lips as he waved the smoke away from his face.

Pretending not to notice, Shikamaru replied with a grin, "It's a celebration cigarette for getting that hassle crossed off the list, you know?"

"Wait, whoa." Naruto waved his hands in protest. "You actually put more hassles on that list, though."

"So this is just 'cause we got more hassles then."

"That's not even an excuse."

"Guess not." Smiling, he finished the second cigarette. And then he started a counterattack. "Here you are giving me flak for smoking, but aren't you going for ramen a lot more than before you got married?"

"Hngh…"

"You're using late night work as an exccuse to go to Ichiraku, like, every day. You gotta face facts, friend. We're both getting to the age where you get a belly. And a fat Hokage, that's not a great look."

"I-I'm still training," Naruto protested. "Believe it. I make sure to burn off what I eat in ramen, so it's all good."

"Really?"

"P-probably…"

"You're hopeless." Shikamaru laughed. In his hand, a third cigarette.

"I just told you you're smoking too much!"

"Shut up. This from the gluttonous Lord Seventh."

"You're the one who needs to shut up!"

"I'm just telling it like it is."

They laughed briefly before settling down again. They looked down on the village of Konohagakure spread out beneath them.

"I'll go to the Land of Fire's daimyo," Naruto said, finally. "You'll come too, yeah?"

"Of course."

"A summit for the daimyo of the five great nations. Gotta make it happen."

"Really leverage that debt he owes us for saving Tento," Shikamaru told him. "If it's hard for you to say, I can do it."

"I know you're ready for that. I'll try a bit harder, too."

"I'm counting on you, Lord Hokage."

"When you call me 'lord,' it feels patronizing."

"It's all in your head. Just your imagination running wild."
He patted Naruto on the back twice, tossed his cigarette in the
ashtray, and turned around. "About time to get to work."

"We're not done talking here!"

The voice of the Hokage at his back sounded innocent in a
way that reminded him of when they were kids.

Shikamaru's face tightened sternly in preparation for their
next battle.

6

"So what exactly are you trying to do here?"

After a late arrival, Madoka Ikkyu, daimyo of the Land
of Fire, sat down across the table from Naruto on the leath-
er sofa. A few days earlier, Ikkyu had come to the village of
Konohagakure for a meeting with Naruto. Now this was their
second meeting in less than ten days. But this time, Naruto
and Shikamaru had gone to the Land of Fire in secret and
were meeting in an unofficial capacity. Ikkyu's residence
had been chosen as the venue. Given the large number of
people who came and went on a daily basis from the daimyo's
residence, no one would notice them as long as they were
disguised. Ikkyu had proposed this plan after giving careful
consideration to the specific needs of this meeting.

So Naruto and Shikamaru had slipped into the residence
alongside some people carrying meat into the kitchen. Now
they sat beside each other facing Ikkyu.

Ikkyu stared at Naruto and began to speak. "You said by
any means possible. So I assume it's quite serious?"

"Yes." Naruto nodded, his face grim.

"Before we get to that, I have to say a word of thanks." Ikkyu held up a hand. "I'm truly grateful your son saved Tento. That group of bandits Mujina are famously fiendish. I don't know what they would have done to my son if the situation had dragged on... When I think about that, I can't thank your son enough. Honestly, thank you." Ikkyu bowed his head of swept-up hair deeply.

"Just stop that," Naruto said. "You don't need to thank us."

"If there's something I can do, just name it. I'll help you insofar as I can."

These words were the reason Shikamaru had done what he had. *Here's where we strike the first blow.*

As if reading Shikamaru's mind, Naruto put his hands on his knees and leaned far forward as he started speaking to Ikkyu. "It's about the matter with the Land of Earth I reported to you the other day."

"Mm-hmm. I also think the situation is alarming. I'll get in touch with the Land of Earth right away and try to dig up the truth."

"That'll be too late." Naruto gave voice to Shikamaru's thought.

His plan rejected, Ikkyu arched an eyebrow slightly, but the young Hokage paid no mind. "According to intel that came into Konoha after our meeting, the ninja of Kumogakure are starting to gather in the village in preparation for the attack on the Land of Flowers. When the Land of Earth invades, Kumogakure will head out immediately. If that happens, then two of the five great nations will end up at war. Three if you count Kirigakure, which has joined up with Iwagakure. Konoha will be dragged into conflict again."

"I understand that we're facing a crisis here," the daimyo agreed. "Which is why I said I would get in touch with the Land of Earth, isn't it? We send a group of observers, and the Land of

Earth won't make any careless moves while they're there. We can buy some time, get proof that they do intend to invade the Land of Flowers, and then censure them for an illegal attack."

"If the Land of Earth forces the attack, a group of observers won't make one bit of difference," Shikamaru interjected. Ikkyu shot him a dissatisfied look, but Shikamaru continued nonetheless. "The Land of Earth is well aware this is an illegal attack. That's why they forced the Tsuchikage to make a demand at the meeting of the Five Kages that would cause a rupture in the Kages' relationship. It's precisely because they know the attack is unjustifiable that they're afraid everyone around them is an enemy. They've likely been laying the groundwork for a while without us realizing it. It's best to assume that they got to work on winning over Kirigakure in the fairly early stages. The situation is already nearing its endgame. We can have the little bit of theater by sending a group of observers, and they'll be treated quite nicely before being sent back—that's about it. During that time, though, the Land of Earth will still be hard at work preparing for their war. It's more than possible that the Land of Earth and Iwagakure will make their move while your observers are still on the road home."

"You... Shikamaru, was it?" Ikkyu asked, scowling.

Shikamaru answered with a nod. He didn't have time to make nice with the daimyo.

"Haste makes waste, as they say. If we anger the Land of Earth by pushing too hard, we lose everything, don't we? I think the most crucial thing is to see how far we can get through peaceable negotiations."

"We passed that point a long time ago."

"Shikamaru..." Naruto's calm voice checked him as he was on the verge of indignation.

After taking a deep breath through his nose, Shikamaru continued, maintaining his calm. "The way things are now, the war will start before ten days are out. Unless we make a more direct move than attempting to curb them with a group of observers, we can't break out of this deadlock."

"You say a direct move. I assume you have a strategy then?" Ikkyu asked.

"The Land of Fire boasts the greatest national power of the five great nations," Shikamaru replied coolly. "We'd like you to draw attention to that power on all fronts and demand a meeting of the daimyo of the five great nations."

"A-a meeting of the daimyo of the five great nations…" Ikkyu was at a loss for words.

Shikamaru pressed on. "Until now, the daimyo of the five great nations have only come together to meet a handful of times in the long history of the continent. The last meeting was in the time of my great-grandfather. But that also means that it's not without precedent. You've had meetings via screens before, too. If the Land of Fire's daimyo sets it in motion, the Land of Earth will have no choice but to go along with it."

"So that includes a threat then."

"Of course." Shikamaru nodded.

Ikkyu gulped audibly. "Are you saying the Land of Fire should make an enemy of the Land of Earth?"

"At best, you have to make it look like that. If they refuse this meeting, who knows where will things go? I'd like you to make your threat clear to the Land of Earth to force them into the meeting venue."

"I'm asking you this, too. We have to do something to stop the war." Naruto grabbed Shikamaru's shoulder. "This guy's been desperately racking his brains, focused exclusively on that. A meeting of the daimyo of the five great nations is for the sake of peace. Shikamaru's always ten steps ahead. He's thinking ahead to what happens after the end of the meeting. I'd appreciate it you'd accept his request."

He bowed his head to the daimyo for Shikamaru's sake. Here Naruto was saving *him* when Shikamaru was the one who had vowed to support the Hokage. His heart grew hot. The academy dropout and the kid who couldn't be bothered had become such ninja that they were facing the daimyo of the Land of Fire for the sake of peace in all nations.

Thanks...

But this feeling of gratitude wasn't just for Naruto. It naturally rose up in him toward his master, his comrades, all the people of the village, and the fact that he was living here and now.

"If you can bring the daimyo of the Land of Earth to the table, you can censure him directly," Shikamaru said. "Of course, the Land of Lightning won't sit by quietly either. If the five daimyo open up and talk honestly, seeking peace, we will absolutely be able to avoid this war. To that end, we ask you to lend us your strength, Lord Ikkyu!"

He got off of the sofa onto his knees, pressed his hands to the floor, and bowed his head. He'd bow this cheap head for however long it took. It was an easy ask if it meant they wouldn't lose this chance. He couldn't let the road to peace be cut off. No matter how narrow and dangerous, he would forge ahead no matter what.

"Stop with the ugly scene."

Does this scene look ugly? Shikamaru wondered. *Is the sight of me fighting that awful? That's fine. There's no need for you to understand me. But...*

"I won't move until you agree," Shikamaru told him. "You said so yourself, Lord Ikkyu, that you would do anything you could. If you do feel the slightest bit indebted to Konoha, please pay it back to us now. I'm asking you. No matter what else happens, we have to make this meeting happen. Somehow."

It would have been easy to ensnare him and force him to agree. If he wanted to make the daimyo do as he asked, he could use an ocular ninjutsu. But if he took control of Ikkyu, the seams would show at the meeting. And the group of daimyo wouldn't be moved by empty words. Ikkyu himself had to consent from his heart or else there was no point. Which was why Shikamaru was facing off with Ikkyu like this from the bottom of his own heart and soul. It was a method for which he was ill-suited. But it was the only way.

"Please." Naruto also got down on his hands and knees next to him.

"Whoa, whoa, now the Lord Hokage..." Ikkyu was clearly flustered.

"I've never seen this guy do this before," Naruto said. "Believe it. He always handles things with a clever quip and a cool face. And now he's here with his head pressed against the floor, not caring how it looks. Please, we need the five daimyo to meet. I want you to move the daimyo of the Land of Earth!"

"Well, you've really got me here." Ikkyu sank deep into the sofa and shrugged. "I suppose this means that I've got to steel myself to jump on this ship with you then."

"If a war starts, there won't be anything to steel yourself about," Naruto noted.

"I suppose. It might be just as you two are saying. If war starts tomorrow, things will get very serious very quickly before I can get a handle on the situation. And it will be too late for regrets when that time comes, hm?"

"Yes," Shikamaru answered.

Ikkyu laughed over him. "I owe a debt to your son Boruto that I can never repay. But if it means I can pay even the smallest part of that debt, I should help you, shouldn't I? No..."

Ikkyu stood up and came around the long heavy table before crouching down between the two men with their heads pressed to the floor.

"I've pushed the Hokage and his capable counselor to this. Let's stop with tepid words like 'help'. Let me fight together with you."

A surprisingly soft and very warm hand touched Shikamaru's back.

Let me fight together with you.

It was a response beyond his wildest dreams.

IN THE TRENCHES

SHIKAMARU'S STORY: MOURNING CLOUDS

1

For the first time in a long time, he had supper at home. He
had a while yet before he got in the bath. Temari had softened
somewhat from the immediate aftermath of the anniversary
incident, but she some coarseness lingered because Shikamaru hadn't made any attempt to bridge the distance
between them while he was running around busy at work.
From where he sat at the table, he looked over his shoulder at
her back as she stood at the sink washing dishes.

What can I say to her?

Should he tell her he was sorry about the whole thing?
No. He'd only make things worse if he brought it all back up.
Maybe he should casually start talking to her like nothing
had happened. But if she demanded to know why he was
suddenly acting so friendly, he'd be stuck for an answer. He
wished—painfully, keenly—that he hadn't forgotten to buy

those flowers from Ino. And Ino knew he was buying them to apologize to Temari, so she wouldn't do anything so tactless as deliver them to the house just because he forgot to take them with him. She would wait for Shikamaru to show up at the store again.

Mind stuck in this endless chain of nonsense, Shikamaru turned his eyes toward the open window. Shikadai was sitting on the veranda, playing video games as he basked in the warm evening sun. Shikamaru didn't know the name of the console or the game. Shikadai was already earning his own money, and as long as he didn't blow it on junk, Temari didn't say anything to him about what he spent it on. He hadn't heard his wife yelling about their son's spending or heard a word about what he was buying, so he figured that Shikadai was making do in his own way.

"Take care of one thing at a time then?" Shikamaru murmured too quietly for either his wife or his son to hear and let out a short sigh before standing up. He slowly approached Shikadai and sat down beside him without saying a word.

He peered at the console screen. A formidable giant of a man in armor was fighting some weird creature. The mechanical clash of battle assaulted his ears. All of Shikadai's fingers were in constant, quick motion. Each time he pressed a button, the large man on the screen swung his weapon violently.

"You like this stuff?" he asked.

"Mm. You know," Shikadai offered, sounds that could be taken as neither confirmation nor denial. He probably couldn't focus on anything else at the moment. He certainly didn't look like he had the bandwidth to be answering questions from his dad.

For a while, Shikamaru sat quietly and watched the game play out on screen.

Every time the man lunged brutally, his son yelped, "Oh!"

or "All right!" He was really focused on this thing. The game was the world; Shikamaru and everything else were invisible to him.

Now that he thought about it, when he was playing a game of shogi against a strong opponent, there were times when Shikamaru stopped seeing the world around him too. And it wasn't just sight: his auditory circuits would forget to do their job, and the whole of his being would be focused on thinking about where to make his next move. The only thing his eyes took in were the pieces on the board before him. He would even lose sight of his opponent at times. There had been times when he was so focused on a game that the world went dark and silent around him until he was shaken back to awareness by his opponent.

Is this in our blood too? Shikamaru wondered as he watched his son smashing the buttons hard enough to break a finger.

"Ngah!"

The armored man, beaten bloody, finally fell. Shikadai cried out in frustration and threw his hands up. He almost tossed the game console out into the garden, but stopped himself before he broke the machine and let out a long sigh.

"Dammit! I was doing super good, too. There's no boost there. Now I have to start over. What a drag," his son muttered, shoulders slumping in disappointment.

"Is it that much fun, that thing?" Shikamaru said.

"Well, you know," Shikadai answered as he finally noticed his father's presence again. "My friends play it too, so it's a drag if I don't get my level up."

"You play because your friends play?"

"That's not what I mean," his son replied, puffing his cheeks out ever so slightly. He set the console down between them and sat back, propping himself up with his hands.

"So then what?" Shikamaru pressed.

"If you mean is it the most fun I've ever had or something, then I guess not. I don't feel like it's that great. Actually, lately I've been playing it out of sheer inertia."

He sounded so much more mature now. Although he was still young enough to be called a child, he was fighting as a full-fledged ninja. Maybe it was only natural that he would be able to dig more deeply and investigate his thoughts more thoroughly than other children.

"So you do it out of inertia?"

"Well, there's no end to this game, so." Shikadai nodded.

"No end?" Shikamaru arched an eyebrow.

"If you change out your equipment, then even the same quest—"

"H-hang on a second there. What's a quest?"

"A mission," Shikadai answered, an annoyed scowl on his face.

"I see," he said, and his son continued with what he had been saying before Shikamaru interrupted.

"The level of difficulty changes depending on your equipment and affiliation, so it's not like you can win if you just get your level up. And this game isn't actually about finishing, really."

Isn't the point of playing a game to finish it? Shikamaru cocked his head to one side. "So what do you do when you don't finish it?"

"You have fun on the quests. When a group of us get together and play, it's different from playing by yourself. You get to hang out and help each other with stuff, which is fun. And when you play solo, you can grind and stuff so you're ready to play with your friends. But when you're alone in a fight you could only do in multi—"

"Multi?"

"Play with everyone else."

Shikamaru dipped his head a little in apology for interrupting, and Shikadai continued.

"When you're alone and you still manage to take down an enemy you could only defeat in multi before, it feels pretty sweet."

"Huh. So then you *do* have fun with it?"

"I guess," Shikadai said and laughed.

The game lecture ended, and the conversation petered out. Silent, father and son looked out on the twilight-colored garden.

Shikamaru broke the silence with the words he had readied earlier. "About that S-rank mission."

Shikadai listened silently. Shikamaru saw that his son was not rejecting him or this conversation like he had the other night wrapped in his futon with his back turned, and so he mustered up the courage to continue. "I heard about what happened. Looks like you had to deal with a hassle on account of me."

His son remained quiet.

"Sorry about that."

"You don't have to apologize, Dad."

Shikadai was exactly right. The fact was this client had tried to get close to Shikadai with their eye on Shikamaru. And Shikamaru had had absolutely no idea that any of it was going on. He wasn't directly involved.

"I never dreamed that my position would have an impact on you," he said. "My very existence has cast a shadow on your ninja path. I can't not apologize for that."

"Cast a shadow on my ninja path?" Shikadai smiled, still looking out into the garden. His smile seemed almost sad somehow. "It's not such a big deal as all that. An S-rank mission out of the blue, it was just too much of a drag, so I said no. That's it."

"A drag, huh?"

"Yeah, total drag. Basically. Just 'cause I looked good in the chunin exams, all these people come out of the woodwork and make this huge fuss over me. But I'm totally not that great. If it means more headaches and more hassles, then I'd rather not be a chunin at all."

"I know a guy who used to think the same thing."

"Who?"

Shikamaru pointed to himself.

"You, Dad?" Shikadai's eyes opened wide in surprise.

Maybe he couldn't imagine Shikamaru like that, given how hard he worked now, how much hassle he willingly took on. But his own boyhood had been one of annoyance at anything and everything, of satisfaction with middling results. That old Shikamaru had still had a dream, though: the dream of a just-right life.

"And I was way worse than you." He smiled as he spoke. "At any rate, doing anything at all was a total drag, and *just right* was basically good enough for me. My dream was to live a lazy, just-right life and then die. I wasn't interested in standing out at all, and I never dreamed of trying to get ahead. If anyone complimented me, I'd always brush it off with 'what a drag.' Anyway, my whole life revolved around trying desperately not to get dragged into any fresh hassles."

"Really?"

"I'm your dad," he told his son. "You get that personality from me. Makes sense when you think about it like that, I bet."

It was a curious logic, but it did make sense. Shikadai could only nod in agreement.

"But..." As the empty sky darkened into night, he saw a vision of his comrades there, injured during the mission to bring back Sasuke. "All that annoying stuff I tried to run from changed me. I always wanted to turn my eyes away from every hassle that popped up before me, but I couldn't. And every time I overcame one, this feeling grew stronger inside of me, like I couldn't just keep drifting along the way I was. I started to feel like I had to stand and face whatever came at me without averting my eyes, no matter how much of a drag it was. I felt like if I did that, I'd be able to find my true self."

"So then the old you wasn't the real you?"

"At the time, I thought it was. I thought strolling along through a just-right life was *very* me, but it looks like I was wrong. Now, though, I can hold my head high and say *this* is the real me."

Shikadai stayed silent. He pursed his lips like he was thinking hard about something. Shikamaru gently touched his back, suddenly noticing how much larger it was.

"I still say things are a drag, though, don't I?"

His son nodded.

"But it means something different now," he said. "When I was a kid, I said everything was a drag without actually putting any real thought into it. But that's not how it is now."

"How is it now?"

"You have to be ready to put your life on the line for whatever it is before you can call that thing a drag. You can't use the word as an excuse to run away. Once you admit that it's a serious drag, you have to do whatever it takes to overcome it. Otherwise, this little verbal tic of ours is just a convenient means of escape."

"You have to be ready to put your life on the line for whatever it is before you can call that thing a drag," Shikadai repeated slowly.

"That's right."

His son took a deep breath and then stood up as he exhaled. He looked down on his still-seated father and smiled shyly. "Teach me shogi sometime."

"What a drag."

Father and son smiled at each other, and the son gave the father a playful look. "I'm gonna jump in the bath."

"You bet."

Shikadai headed back to his own room.

"Woh-kay," Shikamaru muttered to himself, and then looked back into the living room. "Whoa!"

At some point, Temari had come to sit at the low table. She'd apparently overheard their conversation just now.

"What a drag...hm?" she said slowly, staring at Shikamaru with cold eyes.

Without moving from the veranda, Shikamaru waited for his wife to speak.

"Do you remember the first time you asked me out on a date?" She was talking about the Land of Silence. Shikamaru had asked Temari out after the mission. "Do you remember my answer?"

"What a draaaag," he replied immediately.

And for the first time in a long time, Temari smiled at him. "An uninspired phrase, but I think it's a good one."

Shikamaru looked away, embarrassed. He chuckled quietly before once again turning his eyes toward his wife. "What a drag."

The couple laughed together.

2

Shikamaru and Naruto kept their focus on the five men on the screen. They were the masters of the powerful countries known as the five great nations. Some were dignified, some looked so seedy it called into question whether or not they were really masters at all. Each was of different age and appearance. But there was no mistake that these men on the cold, clear screen held the power to change the fate of the continent.

"I thought this would be the issue," said a fat man in his fifties sitting on the right edge of the screen, his dissatisfaction clear on his face. He spread his hands out toward the ceiling and shook his head from side to side in an obvious bit of theater.

The daimyo of the Land of Earth, Danjo.

The flesh on Danjo's chin shook, and he glared at Ikkyu as he argued vehemently, "Just because the ninja proclaim their harmony and the five hidden villages have joined hands, why does that mean that we too must march in step with each other? At times, the five great nations fight, at others, we work together—this has been the state of affairs for some time now, has it not? I would appreciate it very much if you could stop meddling in the governments of other countries."

"That attitude of yours right there is a problem," said the man sitting on the left edge of the screen.

The daimyo of the Land of Lightning, Tekkan.

He had been glaring at Danjo since the start of the meeting, his thick arms crossed tightly. Given that he was the daimyo most opposed to the invasion of the Land of Flowers, this was only to be expected. "Our country has had an alliance with the Land of Flowers for generations. I can't sit by quietly and listen to you tell me you knew that and made the decision to invade anyway."

"Now, now!" Danjo cooed. "Your alliance with the Land of Flowers is nothing more than a habit, a connection your ancient ancestors made, is it not? Why must you go to all the trouble of protecting such a relationship? At any rate, I hear that the Raikage is extremely angry about this matter. If you tell him not to oppose us, I believe we could offer some kind of appropriate token of our appreciation. Naturally, *our* appreciation would be a much better bit of business than your alliance with the Land of Flowers. That's what I came here to discuss today."

"I'm not interested in your games!" Tekkan roared, slamming his fist onto the table.

Danjo's bulk shuddered, and a menial smile rose up on his face.

"The current Raikage is a formidable man," Tekkan snarled. "He's even more hard-headed than his predecessor. He wouldn't listen if I told him to hold back. And there's no reason I would tell him to hold back in the first place."

"That is unfortunate." Danjo started to stand up.

"We're not done talking," Ikkyu rebuked him.

"I believe there's nothing left to talk about," Danjo replied, halfway to his feet.

"So you're still determined to carry out your attack?"

Danjo snorted in laughter.

"Sit down. We're here to talk, aren't we?" Ikkyu said. There was an unshakeable light in his eyes. This man stood at the top of the Land of Fire, the strongest of the five great nations, and he had a majestic gravity that was remarkable even among these five men.

Heaving a dramatic sigh, Danjo sat down.

"This is just..." Naruto muttered, staring at the screen from beside Shikamaru. "It was the same at the meeting of the Five Kages. His greed's all over his face. I feel bad for Kurotsuchi having to go along with a man like that."

Shikamaru was of the same opinion. The layers of Danjo's fat body oozed with selfish ego. Most likely, his greed was the driving force behind the planned invasion of the Land of Flowers.

"I'm absolutely not going to let this guy smash our peace. Believe it," Naruto said, slamming clenched fists against his knees.

"Madara and Tobio had ambition, at least," Shikamaru said calmly to his raging friend. "The last great war was the tragedy that came out of their individual ambitions clashing. That war had a just cause. But the really scary thing here is that we've got this guy standing at the top. He doesn't care how many people have to die to satisfy his own greed. A man like that would gladly destroy this peace built on that previous great ambition."

"We totally can't let him do that."

"That's why we talked about this before we came."

"Right."

They kept their eyes glued to the screen.

This daimyo summit was a fight on top of a fight. The Land of Earth had no intention of abandoning its plan to invade, the Land of Lightning was driven by emotion, and the Land of Fire was earnestly seeking a way to get them both to calm down somehow. Water and Wind maintained their neutrality. Their positions slightly different from those of the Five Kages, the daimyo pushed forward with their heated debate.

"We're not getting anywhere. Let's take a brief break," Ikkyu said, suspending the meeting. When the three of them had strategized beforehand, he had agreed to the ninja's request to put things on pause at just the right moment.

Ikkyu came back to the dressing room where Naruto and Shikamaru were waiting.

"It's no use. Danjo's not budging," he said. He sat down on the sofa and cradled his head in his hands.

"If you give up now, it's all over." Naruto leaned across the table toward the daimyo, as if to give the other man strength. "We have to keep pushing ahead here."

"I know that, but I've got no plan for what to do next."

"We have a strategy." Naruto glanced at Shikamaru. When he nodded, the Hokage nodded back. Now was the only chance they'd have to bring up something they'd been discussing for a while. Their thoughts were one. "I'll agree to the Tsuchikage's demand to disclose Konoha's secrets. We use that to standardize the power of each village, make us all equal. If all the villages are on the same level, the others won't fear Konoha anymore."

"It's not enough," Ikkyu muttered, head still in his hands. And then he lifted his face and looked at the speechless Naruto. "That might be plenty if this were a summit of the Five Kages. But the daimyo won't accept it. I can say we'll level our military might by disclosing Konoha secrets, but Danjo just wants the Land of Flowers."

A pawn that can move the daimyo…

Shikamaru gritted his teeth. Ninja that he was, he didn't have any piece that powerful. They had a plan. But that path was for the daimyo to take, and the ninja Shikamaru had absolutely no say in it.

Looking at the dumfounded pair of ninja before him, Ikkyu closed his eyes and took a deep breath. He expelled all the air in his lungs before nodding deeply once more. "All right. I've decided."

Naruto and Shikamaru said nothing as they waited for Ikkyu to continue.

"There are several enclaves within the domain of the Land of Fire. Fortunately, there's an area my grandfather took near the border with the Land of Earth that doesn't fall too short of the Land of Flowers. The area was originally Earth's. Even now, the people who reside there consider themselves to be citizens of the Land of Earth in their hearts. I'll cede it to him."

"Cede…" Shikamaru murmured.

A broad smile rose up on Ikkyu's face.

"Please wait a moment!" Shikamaru shouted, slapping his hands on the table between them. "Ceding territory's the same as admitting defeat. It means that the Land of Earth defeated us without a fight."

"True." Ikkyu held up a hand to stop Shikamaru. "It's just as you say, the act of giving territory to another country perhaps does mean defeat. But I think it's also better for the people who live in that distant region if we return it to the Land of Earth. I've thought that for some time now. There's nothing for you to worry about."

"But…"

"I said I would fight together with you two," Ikkyu insisted. "Once I decided to fight, I had to prepare myself for the worst."

Shikamaru grew tense in the face of Ikkyu's obvious determination. He set his mind working at top speed in order to respond to this determination and slowly said, "The five great nations alone cannot decide on a matter such as the ceding of land. This will also have an effect on the neighboring smaller countries."

"True. It will." Ikkyu nodded.

"Let's have a grand summit and invite key personnel from all the countries on the continent, not just the daimyo but also their aides," Shikamaru continued. "Naturally, we'd also invite representatives from the land to be ceded."

Their original plan had been to offer the secrets of the village of Konohagakure as a trade for calling off the invasion. But Ikkyu's decision brought them the power to push this idea to a whole other level.

"There's no precedent for a thing like that," the daimyo protested.

"There doesn't have to be," Shikamaru countered.

"The Land of Fire is the most powerful country on the continent, and it is about to cede territory without a fight. This decision affects every nation. The deal should only go ahead with the agreement of all daimyo, their aides, and the people of the land to be ceded."

"Hmm." Ikkyu looked at the table and fell into thought.

Shikamaru had had these words in his head for a while, and now he finally uttered them out loud. "A continental summit!"

Ikkyu gasped, and then he half-muttered, "A continental summit. Can we really pull it off? I honestly have no idea."

"If you decide something's impossible before you even start, you'll never get anywhere," Shikamaru said.

"But some things are indeed impossible—"

"First, let's talk with the daimyo of the five great nations." Shikamaru wouldn't budge. "If that fails, we can think about our next step then. My head is full of different strategies!"

"This is the last card we have to play to avoid a war," Naruto finally said, lending his support to Shikamaru's plan. "Please, I'm begging you."

Shikamaru also bowed his head.

After a period of silence, Ikkyu stood up. "It might be worth a try at least."

The ninja kept their heads bowed until the aura of the daimyo was gone.

The other daimyo were speechless after Ikkyu made his proposal.

"Cede the territory?" Tekkan asked, his right eyebrow arched into a neat semicircle.

"Yes." There was no hesitation in Ikkyu's reply. He nodded at Tekkan and then immediately turned his gaze on Danjo. "It's slightly smaller than the Land of Flowers, but you'll be able to grow crops and other things. How about it, Lord Danjo? Can we make a deal here?"

"B-but the preparations for the attack are already underway." Danjo's chins wobbled. "I've spent a lot of money on this."

"This way means fewer sacrifices," Ikkyu said, smoothly. "Otherwise, you risk the Land of Lightning joining this war, so that you all end up killing each other on a large scale. I don't think what I'm offering is such a bad deal."

"No, but—!" Danjo obstinately rejected the proposal. He was losing the chance to bring down the hammer he'd raised. "What are the Land of Fire and Konoha planning?! Seducing me with sweet words like *cede*? What exactly are your intentions?"

"I simply want to stop a war," Ikkyu insisted.

"You're lying!" Danjo leaped to his feet, shaking his head. Beads of sweat popped up on his round forehead. He flailed as he yelled, "I will not accept this!"

"In that case, we have no other choice. We'll have to ask everyone else," Ikkyu said, coolly.

Tekkan was paying close attention to this exchange, his arms still crossed. The solution to their problem was in the hands of Ikkyu and Danjo now.

"W-what do you mean, 'everyone else'?" Danjo frowned.

"The daimyo of all the countries on this continent and their aides," Ikkyu replied.

"How would we do a thing like that?"

"We all sit down and talk to each other." Ikkyu opened his eyes wide. "A continental summit!"

"A-a continental summit..." Danjo's face, which had been overly confident, now twisted into a menial smile.

"We hold a continental summit and together discuss the Land of Fire's ceding of territory against the Land of Earth's invasion of the Land of Flowers. How does that sound?" Ikkyu smiled.

"Ikkyu, you..." Danjo's selfishness spilled out into his words.

Forced to breath deep of the noxious air of the Land of Earth's daimyo, Ikkyu did not so much as flinch. "If you say you refuse, well, I have some ideas of my own, you know."

The Land of Fire would become the Land of Earth's enemy.

Danjo looked like he would succumb at any moment to the pressure of Ikkyu's implicit threat.

"Sounds like a fine idea, hm?" Tekkan interjected deliberately. Glaring at the Earth daimyo's sweaty round face, the Lightning daimyo continued, "The Land of Lightning agrees to Lord Ikkyu's proposal."

"I do, as well." The daimyo of the Land of Wind raised his hand.

"Then so shall we." The daimyo of the Land of Water followed suit.

"So then, what will you do?" Ikkyu asked, and Danjo no longer had any means of resisting.

3

So much arrogance…

He'd finished work in the middle of the night again, but he still didn't feel like going home. To release the heat trapped inside him, Shikamaru let his feet carry him to the empty forest. The moon hung in the sky, full tonight. The silhouettes of shadows popped up crisp and clear at his feet.

He wove his sign, the sign he had woven since he was a small boy, far too many times to count. When he crossed both arms, his hands took on the shape before the thought had time to reach his conscious mind. He allowed his chakra to accumulate in the pit of his stomach and released it all at once.

The shadow at his feet shuddered and stretched out to the tree ahead of him. Now transformed into an inky black snake, the shadow crawled along the navy-blue ground, and when it reached a thick trunk with exposed roots, it began to climb, winding its way around the tree. When it got to the place where branches stretched out in all directions, the chakra that filled the shadow suddenly grew stronger, and the shadow began to tighten around the dark blue trunk. The tree squealed and creaked. When he infused the jutsu with maximum chakra, Suffocating Darkness would have an effect on physical objects.

Not enough… It's still not enough.

He pushed every scrap of chakra he could muster into the shadow. The tree trunk shrieked. Unable to withstand the pressure of the shadow, the wood started to split in places.

And…

He cut off the flow of chakra, and the shadow that snaked around the tree vanished like mist. A fatigue almost too much to endure overcame him.

"Phew." He kneeled down with a heavy sigh.

More than ten years had passed since he had left the frontlines of battle. His jutsu had languished to the point where he couldn't even smash a single tree. Pathetic, if he did say so himself. When he thought about what would have happened if Naruto hadn't let his anger carry him away at the meeting of the Five Kages and broken Shikamaru's Suffocating Darkness, he shuddered. Just imagining his chakra running out, the jutsu disappearing to leave behind only the animosity of everyone gathered there, the sub-zero icy air of the venue, Shikamaru could hardly stand it.

He sometimes had the thought that it wasn't supposed to have been like this. He was supposed to have carried out just-right missions, married the just-right girl, and lived with their just-right children, followed by a just-right death. That had been the ideal of his childhood.

But reality had led Shikamaru to an unexpected place. A job that was wasted on him, a wife who was wasted on him, a child who was wasted on him... He had it too good.

Worrying that it was too much for him was a luxury; Shikamaru himself knew that better than anyone. Even so, sometimes he longed for that other life, the lazy, laid-back life. The life with no real worries, the one where he grumbled about his just-right wife over a drink with a friend on his way home after a just-right mission, and then took a look at the faces of his sleeping just-right children once he got home before going to bed satisfied. Rinse and repeat. At some point, he'd get old and die with just the right amount of satisfaction. His heart would have been a whole lot lighter if he'd lived *that* life instead of this one.

What a drag what a drag what a drag what a drag...

"What a drag!" he shouted. He clutched at the ground and dug up the earth with his fingers. He was about to be crushed under this pressure.

"Strange," a voice said, and he lifted his eyes from his hands. At some point, a figure had appeared behind the tree he'd been strangling.

All in black...

"I suppose no one in the village knows you get like this."

The shadow slowly drew near and was gradually lit up by the moon: black hair, black cloak. Cold eyes in a pale face looked down on Shikamaru.

"You're back already?" Shikamaru asked.

The man nodded wordlessly.

Uchiha Sasuke. Naruto's rival and best friend. His older brother had killed his entire clan when he was younger, and he'd left the village seeking revenge. Right up until the final stages of the Fourth Great Ninja War, he had walked a different path from Shikamaru, Naruto, and their comrades, moving together with the Akatsuki who'd started the war against the Five Kages. In the last part of the great war, however, Sasuke had fought alongside Naruto, and it was no exaggeration to say that the conflict had ended due to the combined might of Naruto and Sasuke. The two ninja had then reconciled after a one-on-one fight. Now Sasuke was a Konoha shinobi. But his actions during his time as a rogue ninja were far from deserving of praise. He'd fallen so low that at one point his name was in the Bingo Book, a serious criminal. Now he refused to work openly for the village, instead wandering the continent and undertaking missions as the Hokage's shadow.

"I was just on my way to see Naruto," Sasuke said.

This was the last person Shikamaru would have wanted to witness this ugly moment of his. Yanking up whatever meager energy he had in his core, he stood and faced Sasuke.

"Looks like rough times," Sasuke remarked coolly, looking at Shikamaru out of the corner of his eye.

Shikamaru frowned. "We called you back because the situation's dicey as all get-out."

Ro and Soku had reported that Iwagakure was now ready to send ninja into the Land of Flowers the moment the signal was given. Given that the village was essentially on red alert, it was dangerous to simply leave his Anbu in Iwagakure, and so he had already brought them back to Konohagakure.

"They passed through Kumogakure on their way home and found a pretty good number of ninja there too," Shikamaru said. "Darui clearly intends to move fast, whatever happens."

"I see."

If the continental summit broke down, it would mean war. Konoha needed to ready itself for that moment too.

Sasuke's power rivaled that of Naruto, so when Konoha did eventually intervene in the fighting, they would need him on the front lines.

"I pray that I won't have to act," Sasuke said.

"We're working as hard as we can right now so that you won't."

Now that he thought about it, he'd never really talked with Sasuke like this, just the two of them. Back at the academy, he hadn't really liked Sasuke, the way he'd gotten top grades, everyone fussing and fawning over him, and Sasuke taking it all as his natural due. Shikamaru'd never been directly confrontational with him the way Naruto had, though. He hadn't actually wanted to get near to him, so it was more like he almost ran from the other boy. After they became ninja, they both grew busy with missions and had even fewer opportunities for conversation than they'd had at school. When Sasuke left the village, Naruto may have wanted to bring him back to fight together once more, but Shikamaru simply drew a line in the sand—Sasuke was at best a rogue ninja. Thinking about it now, Shikamaru had never once tried to understand him.

"I've been watching events unfold the whole time from far off," Sasuke said, staring at the shadows of the leaves flickering on the ground.

Shikamaru waited quietly for him to continue.

"Meeting of the Five Kages, summit of the five great nations, and now a continental summit... You were the architect for all of it, yes?"

"I'm not a god. I don't have the power to just pull things like that off."

He'd simply used every piece he'd had at his disposal at each and every opportunity, always choosing what had seemed to be the optimal play. Reality didn't go as smoothly as a game on the shogi board. The pieces he played in the real world had feelings and quickly moved beyond the realm of his expectations. But that wasn't to say that it was all bad. Shikamaru and Naruto's proposal probably wouldn't have moved the daimyo at the meeting of the five great nations. Ikkyu's decisive judgement had saved them by the skin of their noses just when they'd lost all hope of victory. This contest was Shikamaru's current battlefield, all the pieces on the board in motion, their very bodies and souls on the line.

"That might be, but it's because you're here that they've made it this far." Sasuke's tone was curt, but it contained real feeling.

To hide his embarrassment, Shikamaru lowered his face and rubbed his nose.

"That loser's no good without you. The only reason he can stand as Hokage is because you're there to support him."

Loser...

That's what Sasuke called Naruto, apparently an expression of his love. Sasuke could have given Shikamaru a run for his money when it came to pigheadedness.

"Pft!" He burst out laughing.

"What?" Sasuke arched an eyebrow.

Shikamaru rubbed his nose with a finger. "I was just thinking you and I are more alike than I once thought."

"I'm not the quick thinker you are."

"Sure, but you're pretty sharp."

"Sharper than Naruto, anyway."

"You're not wrong there."

They both grinned.

"So?" Sasuke's face grew grim again. "You think it'll work?"

"Dunno," Shikamaru answered honestly. "We've come this far. Now we just have to bet on the continental summit.

Every country's got their own way of thinking about stuff. If they lean toward the side of the Land of Earth's daimyo, it'll be full speed ahead to war, a boulder rolling down a hill."

"And you'll be fine with that?" Sasuke asked. "You look to me like you want a world of peace even more than Naruto does."

I don't know.

But it was true that he was absolutely convinced they could not let the world be dragged into that spiral of sadness once again. He slowly pulled a cigarette out of his pocket and brought it to his lips. A bolt of lightning raced across the tip.

Sasuke. His lightning-generating technique, Thousand Birds.

"Quite a fancy lighter," Shikamaru remarked.

"Special just for today."

Smoke began to drift up from the cigarette.

After inhaling deeply, he let out words together with the smoke. "Naruto's this village's sun. He wants peace more than anyone."

"But he lets his feelings get ahead of him," Sasuke noted. "It's because he has you doing the dirty work behind the scenes that he can hope for that peace."

"I can go as deep into the darkness as I need to so long as he keeps shining," Shikamaru told him.

Eyes lowered, Sasuke smiled slightly. Head still hanging, he opened his mouth almost shyly. "You're not the only one supporting Naruto. I'm here, too."

"He's the Hokage. He can't leave Konoha. He can shine because you're fighting for him outside."

"And by his side, you sink into the shadows so that he can be the light."

We really are alike…

Was that it?

Having smoked the cigarette down to the filter, he put it out and tossed the butt in his portable ashtray, closed the lid, and stretched. "It really helps to hear you say that. Just knowing someone's got my back, I can breathe a little easier while I fight this fight."

"It's the same for me."

Shikamaru felt like he understood Sasuke for the first time.

4

"Today's the Land of Iron. I'll be back in three days," Shikamaru said to Temari, who stood behind him as he slid his arms into the sleeves of his white coat. For once, Shikadai was sitting at the low table today. He seemed somehow different from his usual self, his face tense as he ate his breakfast.

"You got today off?" Shikamaru called to him.

"Yeah." The reply was curt, and his son didn't so much as glance his way. Since they didn't know which way things would play out with the Land of Earth, Konoha was increasing the number of ninja stationed in the village, and the effects of this policy were showing up on the younger ninja already.

But this too would end soon. Either everyone would go back to their regular missions or they would head to the battleground. It all depended on what happened at the continental summit the next day.

Straddling the threshold, about to step out into the hallway, he announced, "Okay, I'm off then."

"Dad." Shikadai voice was strained.

Shikamaru stopped and looked back at his son over his shoulder.

Shikadai kept his eyes on the rice in the bowl he held in his right hand. "What's gonna happen to Konoha? What's gonna happen to us?" The honest anxiety of a child spilled out of him, uncontainable. Shikamaru could hear it in the boy's words.

"Shikadai," he said, putting stress on the last syllable.

His son sat up straighter and looked at him with wide, sharp eyes, so like those of his mother.

Smiling, Shikamaru began to speak. "You've got nothing to worry about. Life'll be back to normal, same as usual, the day after tomorrow. So don't just mess around because you have the day off. Go train with Cho-Cho and Inojin."

Shikadai nodded, his face crumpling like he couldn't decide whether to laugh or cry.

Many ninja already knew what was happening throughout the continent right now. Shikadai and Temari would have had to have been aware of what Shikamaru was up against at the moment, but Shikamaru never spoke about work at home, so Temari and Shikadai had also kept quiet about it.

He went back into the living room, crouched down behind his son, and put a hand on his warm head. Temari watched silently. Shikamaru faced forward as he stroked the boy's hair.

"Your dad is the Lord Seventh's right hand," Shikamaru said. "And he's telling you there's nothing to worry about. We're going to be fine."

"Uh-huh." Shikadai sniffled. He was probably trying not to cry.

Shikamaru tousled his hair before taking his hand away and standing up. "I better get going."

"Dad."

"Hm?"

"It's probably a drag, but keep fighting."

"It is a drag, but I'll keep fighting even if it kills me." He turned his back to his son and walked down the hall. Temari was silent behind him as he sat on the step that led down to the entryway and pulled on his shoes.

"Okay!" He stood up and turned around with a smile on his face. He looked at Temari. She wore her usual tough expression as she returned his gaze. "I'll be back in three days."

Temari nodded. "Never forget that no matter what happens to you, you've got two comrades who would never betray you."

Temari and Shikadai. His priceless family.

Smiling, he nodded. "You don't have to tell me. I know."

"Yeah?"

"Mm."

They smiled at each other.

"Say, Shikamaru?"

"What?"

"I don't care if you don't remember anniversaries and things like that. Well, at the time, I was a little angry, but it's honestly fine either way."

Neither of them was particularly good at saying what they really felt. It was something they had in common. But in that moment, Temari was desperately trying to communicate her feelings to him. And that was enough for Shikamaru. He felt gratified just knowing that Temari would always be upfront and honest with him whatever the words—even if she said she hated him.

Wait...

He'd be in a bit of trouble if she didn't like him a little at least.

Standing in the entryway, Shikamaru waited unhurried for his wife to continue.

"You've never once talked about work at home. I know that's because you don't want to put us through all that. But it's annoying."

It was indeed true that he didn't want to put them through anything painful. But Shikamaru had another reason for not talking about work at home.

He didn't want to be the kind of man who has a couple drinks and grumbles about all the terrible things he has to deal with in the world outside. This wasn't just in front of his family either; he was the same with everyone he saw. Complaining wouldn't move him a single step forward. If he had time to whine about all his problems, then it was by far more constructive to spend that time dealing with them.

It was true that he would occasionally grumble about something or other when he was out having a good time. But those words weren't from his heart. They were jokes, things the people he was with could simply laugh off. It was different from complaining. Or so he personally thought.

"Talk to me," Temari said, her eyes red, bringing to life an old memory in the back of his mind.

It was back when Darui, Kurotsuchi, and Chojuro were still spirited young ninja of their villages. Separate from the meeting of the Five Kages, the up-and-coming ninja of the different villages would sometimes get together in the Land of Iron. Shikamaru and Temari had both been members of that group.

This was around the time he'd snuck into the Land of Silence alone, after it was determined that the reason for the decline in incoming missions lay in that strange nation, and tried to assassinate their leader, Gengo. Shikamaru had headed out on his assassination mission without even telling the people he was close to in Konoha, much less the members of this group in the Land of Iron.

He'd been tense, though. And before anyone else, Temari noticed that Shikamaru was off from his usual self somehow. She'd asked him if she could lend a hand, and he had brushed her off.

"You remember?" he asked the woman who had once been his comrade and was now his wife.

Of course, Temari only cocked her head, not understanding the meaning of his question.

"Before I went to the Land of Silence. You hit me."

When he'd told her he didn't need her help and rebuffed any further inquiry, Temari had knocked him flying. She'd been crying.

"I'm hopeless," he told her. "I'm doing the same thing I did back then."

But now as she was opening her heart to him, his own heart also opened, spilling forth a sentiment and affection he'd never shown anyone before. Eyes bright red, Temari shook her head from side to side. "You're doing plenty. There's no need for me to hit you now. You're a wonderful man."

No one else could have said those words and made him happier than he was now. And he could believe those words coming from her.

It's probably a drag, but keep fighting.

You're a wonderful man.

His son and his wife held Shikamaru up with their loving words. He felt a surge of strength in the core of his heart, and he knew he wouldn't waver no matter what happened in the days to come. This was the best pep talk he could have hoped for heading into the final match.

"Go, Shikamaru. And since you're going, make sure you win. I won't let you through that door again if you lose." Her eyes were still red, but her face was back to the usual Temari.

She despised things being askew and was stricter than anyone with their son. She was too good of a wife for him and a perfect mother.

"It's a drag, but I guess I'll go."

"Get out there."

With warmth in his heart, Shikamaru opened the door that led to the battlefield.

THE FUTURE

SHIKAMARU'S STORY: MOURNING CLOUDS

1

It was an incredible sight, the daimyo and their aides from across the entire continent coming together to meet in a single building. They were separated by country at the ten rows of long semicircular tables arranged in concentric rings. The gazes of some hundreds of people were focused on the podium standing in the center.

The Land of Iron had worked at top speed to build this facility. The daimyo had put up a roof over the plaza where he spoke to his citizens and had exactly enough tables and chairs made specifically for this meeting.

It was an unprecedented summit. It was beyond anything ever seen before from start to finish.

Everyone there was worked up, full of fire before this weaponless battle. The meeting venue, a plaza with nothing more than a roof thrown over it, was exposed to the wind, and despite the cool breeze blowing in from all sides, Shika-maru was sweating.

Seated at the tables closest to the podium were the daimyo and aides of the five great nations. The Five Kages and faces from the hidden villages were in the row directly behind them. Shikamaru was in the section set aside for the village of Konohagakure near the middle of the long table. Beside Naruto, naturally.

"We've finally made it," Naruto whispered to him before the meeting. His blue eyes were focused on the empty podi-um. "Whether we like it or not, this is where it ends."

"Mm-hm." Shikamaru agreed. "If more than half of the countries at this summit agree with the Land of Earth, then it's full speed ahead to war. No one's ever had a meeting like this before. If they get approval here, there'll be no stopping the Land of Earth. They'll pull in the countries that agree with them and invade the Land of Flowers."

"We can't let that happen."

"Of course not." He put his prayer into words.

There was no knowing the results of the meeting until they saw how it all played out. He couldn't predict how many countries would be accepting of Danjo's greed.

The instant the Land of Earth's invasion was approved, they would no longer have the option of a covert attack on Danjo. There were too many countries assembled here to be able to carry out such an operation without suspicion. Not only was the Land of Iron providing security, the Five Kages also shared the responsibility to keep the meeting members safe. If Konoha tried anything funny, they'd be found out right away.

"It's starting."

A samurai sat down at the table next to the podium: the Land of Iron's general. To keep the meeting running smoothly, it had been decided that the general of the Land of Iron, the host country and a neutral party, would act as chairperson.

"We will now convene the continental summit."

At his word, the meeting began.

The chairperson gave a rough summary of the events leading up to the summit, as well as the statements from the discordant parties involved, the Land of Earth and the Land of Fire. The outcome they came to about this matter would change the fate of the continent. The entire audience sat in tense silence as the chairperson spoke.

Once the long explanation was finished, one of the central parties, Danjo was invited to take the podium.

As he stood there with a leisurely smile on his face, Danjo raised a hand toward the assembled members and bowed respectfully. He took a short breath, placed both hands on the podium, and began to speak. "There is a kind of human being on this continent known as the ninja," the daimyo began. "Ninja... From the moment they are born, they are destined to fight. They can only find the meaning of their own existence in battle. They study the art of violence from a young age. They are taught by their parents and instructors to deceive others, and only once they become hardened professionals in battle can they be recognized as full-fledged members of their villages. Many of the people born to ninja in these 'hidden villages' do not doubt from the time of their birth that they will walk the path of the ninja. Even now as we sit here like this, new ninja are being born in every one of those villages."

They only find the meaning of their existence in battle...

Shikamaru couldn't completely deny what Danjo was saying. It was true that somewhere in his heart, he always sought to put himself into the middle of electric battle. That feeling was so deep in his bones, it would have been better to call it an instinct at this point. Most likely, the majority of ninja felt the same as he did.

Only by pushing themselves into extreme situations could they cultivate their jutsu and chakra. Although their individual aims might have been different, ninja walked the path of the ninja. And this was definitely not an evenly paved road. That was why ninja naturally acquired the habit of putting themselves into harsh environments. But did that mean in the end that a ninja's only truth lay in fighting?

No. Shikamaru had a family he loved. He had comrades to protect. He was here in this place now for their sake. He was sitting there to *stop* the fight.

He couldn't deny what Danjo was saying in his head, but he had no intention of simply sitting quietly and agreeing with him.

Oblivious to Shikamaru's thoughts, the massive daimyo of the Land of Earth continued. "The history of the continent has been writ alongside these warriors. I do not intend to condemn them nor suppress them. On the contrary, I more than anyone affirm them and their existence. Which is why I have chosen this path!" Danjo waved a hand high in the air with a theatrical flare.

From beside him, Shikamaru heard a sound like something hard being ground to dust. Naruto was gritting his teeth and glaring at Danjo.

"I do not mean to say this is a matter of survival of the fittest. The Land of Flowers no doubt also has the weapons to stand up and face us. And there are those who would assist them. We do not devour the weak. We fight on equal footing, country to country. The sweet fantasy of peace robs the ninja of their very reason for being. We and the ninja are in a relationship of coexistence. Accepting them means accepting war. Unless we ensure a place for them, those of us who are not ninja will someday be dragged into their delusions just like we were with the previous great war. Is it not time at last for the world to channel their instinct to fight in an appropriate fashion in order to prevent massive chaos, as well as to accept open warfare as we did in the past?!"

"You gotta be kidding me here," Naruto spat, his voice heavy. "He just wants to satisfy his own greed. And then he goes turning that into the meaning of a ninja's existence!"

"Calm down," Shikamaru murmured, touching Naruto's clenched fists.

Danjo finished his speech at last and received a smattering of applause, definitely not from the majority of the audience.

"Next is Lord Ikkyu," Shikamaru said, and Naruto closed his eyes and took a deep breath as he nodded.

Ikkyu took the floor. He did not offer an exaggerated greeting like Danjo had. He simply bowed his head matter-of-factly to the people assembled and thanked them for coming. And then he looked around the room and began to speak, a calm look on his face.

"I would like to ask you." Ikkyu smiled slightly. "Can ninja really only thrive in the throes of battle?" He glanced at Naruto, then raised and lowered his chin slightly, only enough for Naruto and Shikamaru to notice, before turning back to the other attendees. "As I listened to Lord Danjo, I simply couldn't rid myself of this sense of dissonance. Because it sounded to me as though he believes the ninja themselves want to fight. Is that really the case, though, in the end?" Ikkyu paused for a moment. "I can say with certainty that it is not."

Ikkyu's voice was quieter and weaker than Danjo's, which came up from the bottom of his stomach. But the softness of it settled deeply into the entire venue.

"Right now, all the daimyo of the continent are gathered here, regardless of the size of the nation. Rich or poor, strong or weak. We have come together now as comrades, working on behalf of our respective countries. Fortunately, there was not a single daimyo who refused our call to be here today. This is truly unprecedented. Every daimyo on the continent coming together to discuss a single issue. Perhaps some have considered the idea before, but they thought that such a summit would be impossible to realize and so gave up before they had even started. But today, we have made just such a meeting a reality."

Everyone in their room held their breath so as not to miss a single word. Ikkyu's gentle speech had drawn them all in.

"We could not have managed this historic feat without someone making that first move. In fact, the war we discuss would have already started long ago. A month—no, ten days. And if everything failed, even a day ago... I know of someone who has bought us this time, someone who has fought desperately right up to the last second to prevent a war however he could."

Something warm tightened in Shikamaru's chest.

"I am indeed the one who advocated for this meeting. But what I did is truly insignificant. My decision to cede the Land of Fire's territory was a product of watching a man who would fight until the bitter end, someone who would never give up even as he was forced to crawl. Compared with this brave soul, I have done nothing. I have never sweated blood to make something happen the way he has. My father was the daimyo of the Land of Fire. I have merely run along the rails laid out for me. I never thought to fight a stronger power or run the opposite direction on those rails. But I feel that, by watching this man fight, I have changed. Now, I would push back against any rapids, no matter how they raged, if it meant that the world would remain at peace."

Here, at last, Ikkyu raised a hand. His fingers were pointed at Naruto.

"The man who changed me is a ninja. A man who rejected the fight, who fought against war harder than anyone I've seen before. A man who struggled valiantly up to the last moment to avoid a fight. A man Lord Danjo said could only live in the midst of a fight. A ninja."

A clamor rose up in the venue, and Ikkyu was silent for a moment as he waited for it to calm down. He then slowly opened his mouth once more.

"Can we truly say that the only way to fight is by carving flesh and breaking bones? The ninja who has changed my life and my heart is a man who has worked to find his way from one harsh environment to another. And yet no matter how difficult a position he found himself in, even if it was a situation in which your average person would simply give up, he never lost faith in his victory and charged ahead full speed. And this is indeed the figure of a fighter. But his fight did not lead him to blood or tears or bodies in the end. It led him to this summit now. The passionate spirit that lives inside of this ninja does not exist solely for the purpose of hurting others. Now that I myself am changed with him by my side, I can say this with utter certainty." A light shone in the eyes of the Fire daimyo. "It is precisely because the ninja are on the very frontlines of war that they desire peace more strongly than any of us!" Here, Ikkyu smiled. "Rather than me going on at length, there's someone else here who can communicate to you much more clearly what it is I wish to say, so I would like to hand him the baton now. May I do so?"

Applause erupted from the audience.

"Naruto!" Ikkyu called.

Shikamaru's friend stood up beside him, and the applause in the makeshift hall grew even more thunderous.

"I want you to hear what he has to say!" Ikkyu cried, his voice the loudest it had been that day.

Naruto looked at Shikamaru.

He smiled at his partner. "Go on then."

"Yeah."

Naruto stood at the podium vacated by Ikkyu. After watching him go up there, Shikamaru got to his feet.

"What's the matter, Shikamaru?" Mirai asked, a look of surprise on her face when he was about to pass in front of her at the end of the row. "The Lord Hokage is about to speak."

"Cigarette. Going for a smoke. It's no smoking in here, right?"

"At a time like this?" Mirai looked at him contemptuously, and Shikamaru turned his back to Naruto at the podium.

Ikkyu had said he would fight together with them, and of course he had set Naruto at the podium. Shikamaru also thought Naruto should speak if the meeting came to a tense impass. He'd anticipated that Ikkyu would make that happen. In his head, he could clearly see how the game would play out. And Naruto wasn't the sort of man to bungle this. If Naruto spoke, it would all be okay. Shikamaru had an absolute faith in that.

The game was over. There was no longer any need for him to be there.

"Our Hokage is an idiot, but no one can beat him when it comes to heart. Brace yourselves and listen," Shikamaru murmured to the representatives of each country, who were focused on the podium, and left the venue.

His job was done.

2

"I wasn't trying to do anything special."

Even from outside the venue, Shikamaru could hear Naruto loud and clear. Standing beside the cylindrical ashtray, he let the smoke waft out of his mouth as he strained his ears to catch his friend's speech.

He'd never been good at gatherings like this. He had to admit that doing anything in front of a full house was such an unbearable drag, he could hardly stand it. This basic nature of his never changed, no matter how old he got. As the Hokage's advisor, he had set foot in places like this more times than he could count, but deep in his heart, he would always be the boy who thought anything and everything was a drag. Shikamaru could hear that boy cursing about all the annoying things he put them both through.

Being bathed in light was the Hokage's job. Like Sasuke, Shikamaru worked as Naruto's shadow; there was no need for him to sit in that meeting hall.

"We all want a peaceful tomorrow. And lasting peace is just a sequence of those tomorrows, isn't it?" Naruto didn't try to sound fancy or put on airs in front of the daimyo.

The way you are's good enough, Shikamaru thought. People who spoke in lofty tones and pretended to be something they weren't had no passion. Naruto could just be Naruto, the man who had endless, boundless faith in people.

"Families sit around the dinner table, kids go to school with smiles. A ninja's no different from anyone else. Mornings like this are happiness to us, too. We know better than anyone how seriously priceless such uneventful days are after fighting in the Fourth Great Ninja War."

During the war, it hadn't only been the ninja of the five hidden villages who came together under the leadership of the Fifth Hokage, but also the ninja from the smaller nations. All of them had been someone's father, someone's mother—they were all parents and children. So many families who were unknown to Shikamaru had been sacrificed in that war, they had people waiting for them to come home. How great had their grief been when no one returned? Now that he was a parent, the full extent of the tragedy the great war had wrought felt painfully real to him. What would Temari and Shikadai do if they got a notice that he was dead? How would he feel if he found out Shikadai had died in battle?

Just the thought of it nauseated him and made his hair stand on end. He couldn't even stand the mere idea of it. To calm himself down, he lit his second cigarette.

Naruto's speech continued in the hall behind him.

"Lord Danjo said that ninja can only validate their existence in battle, but I'm telling you that's not true. It's precisely because we fight that we want peace. Ninja resist and endure. We never stop believing in the light, never stop moving forward, no matter how tough things get for us. Ninja don't fight to find the meaning of our own existence. We fight because we seek the light. We fight for peace…"

The venue was so quiet, you could hear a pin drop.

That hopeless boy, the academy dropout, had really grown up. Deep in his heart, Shikamaru was proud of Naruto. He was glad he was the Hokage of his generation.

He looked up at the sky. Snowy white clouds drifted along.

Wonder what's happening with the family right now. He very much wanted to see them.

3

Three years or so earlier, a large building had been constructed at the crossroads of the village of Konohagakure's main streets. Once it was completed, a large video screen had been installed on one wall. Most of the time, it showed advertisements for the latest ninja tools or music videos by Land of Fire singers, but that day was different. Today, it showed the hero of the village.

A large crowd had gathered at the crossroads and was looking up at the screen. Shikadai was in their midst, with Cho-Cho standing to his right and Inojin to his left. All three watched the Hokage's speech intently.

On the screen, Naruto said, "There is some truth to what Lord Danjo says."

The continental summit brought together every daimyo on the continent. And before such an impressive gathering of personnel, Naruto stood tall and spoke his mind. Shikadai felt like he belonged to a totally different world.

"Ninja *are* a tool of war. That might be the reality we live in. But if that's the case, then we should not have ninja in this world."

A clamor rose up at the continental summit, which came to them through the screen.

"What's the Lord Hokage talking about?" Inojin muttered. When Shikadai turned his eyes that way, Inojin continued in a reproachful tone, still focused on Naruto, "We're ninja, aren't we? And, I mean, the Lord Hokage… He's a ninja. Ninja shouldn't exist? What exactly is he trying to do?"

But Shikadai basically got what the Hokage was saying without coming right out and saying it. "Isn't that what, like, peace kind of is? You know?"

Perhaps it didn't quite click for Inojin—he merely raised a skeptical eyebrow. Shikadai himself had only the haziest sense of the idea, though, so he wouldn't be able to offer up a better answer even if he kept on trying to put that vague feeling into better words.

"Shut up and watch," he said instead and focused on the screen.

"You're going to vote today on the Land of Fire's proposition to cede this territory to the Land of Earth. But before you do, I have one more proposal to make, this one from the village of Konohagakure." Naruto paused, the span of a single breath.

"So, like…" Cho-Cho said.

Shikadai raised his eyebrows and turned his gaze toward her, wondering what she just had to say right now at such a critical moment.

"So my dad says it was your dad who said we should have this whole summit thing in the first place, Shikadai."

He started, then braced himself so that his comrades didn't notice his surprise.

"My dad looked really happy 'bout the whole thing. He said that if it wasn't for your dad, we woulda gone to war ages ago."

His heart pounded loudly, and goose bumps popped up all over his body.

His dad. The man who spent half his time in the house getting yelled at by Shikadai's mom. Shirt always off, never bothering to take a bath when he came home in the middle of the night. On his rare days off, he'd sit on the veranda and stare vacantly out at the garden. Shikadai might have been his son, but he couldn't help thinking that his dad was a huge mess.

And that *guy was working this kind of massive job…*

He was at a loss for words.

The camera cut from Naruto to show the inside of the meeting hall. Shikadai could clearly make out Mirai and other faces from the village of Konohagakure, but his father wasn't among them. Why wasn't his father there? If what Cho-Cho was saying was true, then there was no way his father wouldn't have been there for the Hokage's speech.

And yet…

His father *had* to have been there. He was no doubt watching over Naruto from some corner of the room that wasn't shown on the screen. Cho-Cho's father had probably been telling the truth about this whole thing.

"You have to be ready to put your life on the line for whatever it is before you can call that thing a drag. You can't use the word as an excuse to run. Once you admit that it's a serious drag, you have to do whatever it takes to overcome that thing. Otherwise, this little verbal tic of ours is just a convenient means of escape."

His father had told him this. He had faith now.

"That's like—Shikamaru's amazing, huh?" Inojin said.

Shikadai couldn't answer his friend. He felt like he'd start crying if he said a word.

4

Alone in the family's living room, Temari watched Naruto on the TV screen earnestly reading from an unfamiliar script.

"We propose to share all intelligence among all the hidden villages and redress differences in individual battle power. As a first step, Konoha will disclose its own secret intelligence to the other villages. If we can make real progress in sharing information with one another, we can create peaceful uses for ninjutsu. With new uses for ninja techniques, ninja can earn their living without having to go on dangerous missions." Naruto lifted his face from his notes. "As Hokage, I want to propose this to all the nations gathered here."

Temari listened solemnly, kneeling before the screen in a formal position. They had shown the inside of the hall a moment earlier, and she found her brothers seated at one table, representatives of Sunagakure. They'd almost been smiling at Naruto on the podium, and she'd breathed a sigh of relief.

But critical member was nowhere to be found: Shikamaru was not sitting with Konoha.

My job's done. It's a drag sitting in a room full of people like that. She could almost hear her husband's voice.

"We absolutely can't go to war. Please, I'm asking you. As representatives of your countries, please make the only rational decision." Naruto bowed so deeply that his head almost rested on the podium.

Temari felt something sublime in the figure he cut. It was a grand speech from the Hokage of Konoha, from a single ninja among many. And at work in his shadow was her husband. He did everything he possibly could for Naruto and for the village of Konohagakure. In fact, it was more than that; that husband of hers squeezed out every last ounce of strength he had for the sake of the whole world.

Shikamaru desperately hoped for peace. He felt more strongly than anyone else that the time of the ninja was over. A lazy life, lazy days, a lazy death—this was what Shikamaru wanted.

Sometimes the thought struck her that maybe she had been the one who had snatched that dream away from him. Had Shikamaru been forced to the frontlines of battle because of Temari and Shikadai, even though he desired nothing other than a life of idleness? Wouldn't he actually prefer to work somewhere more easygoing, a place that didn't cause such waves in his heart?

Temari was a ninja. There had been a time when she was hostile to Shikamaru and Naruto and the rest of them. She had lived as a ninja of Sunagakure and married into the village of Konohagakure. She had her own ninja tools and a very clear idea of what exactly a ninja was and should be. Perhaps she had unconsciously sought that in Shikamaru and Shikadai.

Her husband was the kindest man she knew. For her sake and the sake of her son, for Naruto, for the village of Konohagakure, he always put himself second. He was too good for her. But in his heart, did he actually want to throw it all away and drift along like a cloud, living however he pleased?

She had been too scared to ever ask him. She was grateful to him for working so hard on their behalf, and she had faith in him. No one took greater joy in Shikadai's growth than Shikamaru. After Shikadai's big showing in the chunin exams, he had come home and gleefully described every minute of it to her. Shikamaru was a good father, which was exactly why, when he was in this house, she wanted him to be his true self.

She clenched the hands resting on her knees as she knelt before the TV. Her fingers caught on her thighs, digging into them lightly.

Naruto stepped down from the podium. The hall was enveloped in thunderous applause.

"You really worked hard, huh, Shikamaru?" Temari said to the empty seat next to Naruto as he sat down.

5

I'm falling asleep here.

The smoking area outside the venue was reserved for Shikamaru's personal party of one. Everyone else was utterly swept up by the summit inside, so naturally, no one was tearing themselves away to come out for a cigarette.

Lying on the long bench likely set up there in a hurry before the meeting, he stared absently up at the sky.

Inside, the representatives of the many participating nations were giving their speeches. Before the start of the summit, those who wished to speak had indicated that intention so that they could be allocated a certain amount of time, and they now came to the podium in order, one after the other. All of these arrangements had been splendidly executed by the samurai of the Land of Iron. Their experience in handling Five Kage summits over long years spoke volumes at times like this. And it appeared that any country that applied in advance was being given the opportunity to have their say. The voting probably wouldn't even start until quite late.

"So boring…" How was he going to pass the time until then?

Most of the voices that spilled out from the hall to reach his ears were in agreement with the Land of Fire and Naruto. Some countries even severely censured the Land of Earth. What Shikamaru found deeply strange, however, was the fact that one of the countries at the heart of the matter, the Land of Flowers, was not on the list of speakers he'd seen before the meeting started. They were not going to speak at this critical juncture despite the fact that they were the ones facing an invasion at the unilateral decision of a great nation.

It had been a while now since he'd left the meeting. During that time, the only people who invaded his private smoking space were a couple of samurai on guard, apparently taking a break. Neither of them spoke to Shikamaru sprawled out on the bench in the corner.

A familiar voice drifted out from inside. "I cannot disregard the Hokage's magnanimous concession."

Kurotsuchi. Her voice was as cool and collected as it was when speaking with the Five Kages, despite the much larger platform she had here.

"The inequality in battle power caused by Konohagakure's excessive might will most assuredly become the seed of war.

To protect my own nation, I resolved to accept the Land of Earth's petition and cooperate in the invasion of the Land of Flowers. However, the Hokage's speech today and the brave decision of the Land of Fire's daimyo, Lord Ikkyu, have caused me to realize that the situation that I feared was an evil vision born of my own weak heart. There was absolutely no outside interference such as genjutsu at work when I made my decision. It stemmed entirely from my own weakness."

The self-possessed Tsuchikage looked at even her own self with her sharp, penetrating eyes. She wasn't a stupid ninja. When the situation changed, she was able to pull back on what she had previously asserted in an almost pleasingly refreshing way rather than cling to a foolish agenda for the sake of her ego.

"I would like to accept the petitions of the Hokage and Lord Ikkyu. If these motions are accepted, then the village of Iwagakure will no longer have a reason to fight."

"Yes!" Shikamaru clenched a fist, still lying on his back.

If Iwagakure pulled out, then the Land of Earth would lose the majority of their fighting strength. The five great nations had essentially abandoned their own national armies by relying on ninja over soldiers, and they no longer had the power to go to war on their own. Kurotsuchi's declaration told the entire world that a war had just been averted. There was no longer any need for a vote. The fact that Kurotsuchi had bent decided their victory.

"Fwaaaa." He yawned, assaulted by a sudden sleepiness. Tears filled his eyes and spilled out, sliding down past his ears. It was entirely the fault of this yawn. He definitely wasn't so overcome with emotion that he was crying. He wasn't just playing tough here; these were simply tears brought about by yawning.

All of this—the meetings, the speeches, the maneuvering—it was absolutely a real fight for Shikamaru. A very difficult fight, in fact, one he couldn't even have begun to tackle under his own power alone. Compared with this epic battle, he'd just been playing house on his previous missions.

And this was actually the story of Shikamaru himself. Up until now, the fight had been his and his alone. Although he had worked with his teammates, in the end, he fought directly himself, testing his own abilities. When he was hurt and defeated, he only had his own inexperience to blame. He could have died, and it would have had no effect on the country or public order. No sea of blazing flames would swallow up the continent.

But this time was different. Their loss, of course, wouldn't have meant that Shikamaru died right then and there. As a ninja, his abilities were beyond question. But if they'd lost, the situation would have been much more serious than his own death. A defeat would have led directly to war among the nations, and the grave pressure of that fact weighed more heavily on him than any pressure he'd ever felt before this.

We won…

And yet, strangely, he felt no sense of accomplishment. This was not his victory—it was the world's victory. They had been led to this fortunate result because the people on this continent desired true peace.

"Not too shabby."

He'd given up his just-right life when he decided that he would hold Naruto up. This was Shikamaru's battlefield now. It was a battlefield where he held no sword, where he didn't even use his jutsu. And he himself had chosen to live here, irritated all the while. He had no regrets.

"But, still, it really is a drag," he muttered and smiled.

He didn't feel a sense of accomplishment, but the feeling he did have was all right. The days of quiet tranquility were back. Just the thought of it made his heart grew lighter.

He closed his eyes. The darkness behind his eyelids reached out, intent on sucking him in. Which reminded him that he hadn't been sleeping too well lately. He'd been too on edge to sleep.

Let me sleep today at least.

"…maru."

A voice.

"Shikama…"

Who?

"Shikamaru!"

The world shook violently, and he rolled off of the bench. He looked up with red eyes to find his friend outlined against the night sky.

"Naruto," he murmured, dazed, squatting next to the bench. He'd been having a good dream, but now he couldn't remember what it was. His mind was half-drifting in sleep even now.

The Hokage looked down, exasperation on his face, hands on his hips. "It's over."

"Yeah?"

"You hear the result?"

"Nah."

Hands still on his hips, Naruto sighed.

The moon had risen quite high in the sky. The last quarter looked down on them from its perch in the darkness.

"Not even interested?" Naruto asked, almost sulking.

Shikamaru snorted with laughter and shook his head from side to side.

"Why not?"

"I heard up to Kurotsuchi's speech," he replied and yawned. After wiping away the tears that had welled up in the corners of his eyes, he offered his unconvinced friend some additional words of explanation. "It was obvious that we won the minute she accepted the proposal from you and Lord Ikkyu."

"So that's why you were sleeping out here?"

"Yeah."

"Sounds about right for you." Naruto laughed. "Shikamaru?"

"Yeah?"

"Thanks," he said, a curious look on his face. "I was able to get this far because you were right there with me the whole time. I would've given up ages ago without you."

"Liar." Shikamaru snorted. "You would never have given up, with or without me." The words *give up* weren't actually in Naruto's vocabulary.

"I'm telling ya, I wouldn't have known what to do without you. You always shine a light on the path I'm supposed to follow." His friend held out a hand. "Keep being there for me."

Shikamaru grabbed the offered hand, and a powerful force pulled him to his feet.

"Naruto. Shikamaru," Kurotsuchi called out, approaching them with her aide in tow. Coming to a stop in front of Naruto, the Tsuchikage smiled gently. "I see how far you were willing to go. And I get it. I wronged you. I'm sorry. I just apologized to Chojuro too."

A smile spreading from ear to ear, Naruto shook his head. "You were in a tough spot because of that daimyo, yeah? Don't worry about it."

"I appreciate you saying that." She bowed her head slightly.

"Let's keep things moving forward, Kurotsuchi." Naruto stretched out a hand, and the Tsuchikage gently accepted it with her own. Hands clasped, they smiled at each other for a moment before Kurotsuchi pulled hers away and turned her back to them.

"Oh, right! Shikamaru?" She looked at him over her shoulder. "Be good to Temari."

"I know."

The corners of her mouth curled upward, and then Kurotsuchi left them alone again.

"It's over, huh?" Shikamaru took a cigarette out of his pocket and put it to his lips.

Naruto frowned. "You gotta quit smoking already."

"I'll think about it," he said and lit the cigarette. It tasted better than any cigarette in recent memory. The smoke drifted around him, and the visceral feeling of their victory rose up inside of him. "Should we get back to the village?"

Naruto's shoulders dropped. "We've got a mountain of work to do."

"That's a good thing, though," Shikamaru replied. A vision of the piles of papers popped up in the back of his mind. Instantly, his spirits plummeted. He had no time to delight in their victory.

6

"Thank you so, so much," the daimyo said and bowed his head deeply, so deeply.

Sitting in a chair behind Naruto, who sat across from the daimyo, Shikamaru felt a slight smile playing on his lips.

Despite his long journey to Konoha and having arrived only the day before, the daimyo of the Land of Flowers didn't seem the least bit tired. He was young, the same age as Shika-dai. It turned out that he had only become daimyo six months earlier after his father's sudden passing. Abruptly thrust into the limelight, he had put body and soul into the unfamiliar work when the invasion of the Land of Earth had come like a bolt from the blue.

"My country is truly small. If this had escalated to war, I don't know what would have happened to my people. The citizens of the territory ceded to the Land of Earth were also quite moved by the goodwill of Lord Ikkyu and agreed to the cession. The culture of the Land of Earth has always had strong roots there, so it seems that everyone is happy about this turn of events. Lord Ikkyu says it is all because you and your people worked so fervently on our behalf, Lord Hokage. I can never begin to thank you enough." The boy had not stopped bowing since setting foot into the room.

Naruto scratched his head in embarrassment.

Shikamaru was just plain glad that the people of the land to be ceded had agreed to the deal. And after being showered with criticism and complaint from every country at the continental summit, Danjo had taken well to the task and needs of the citizens in his new territory. The cession had been a success.

The young daimyo was remarkably soft-spoken, much more so than Shikadai and the other young ninja of Konoha.

"Er, I realize this is rude," Shikamaru raised a hand, inter-rupting the conversation.

"What is it, Shikamaru?" Naruto looked over his shoul-der at him. And then, as if remembering something, he turned back to the daimyo of the Land of Flowers and leaned forward. "The meeting of the Five Kages, the continental summit. That whole chain of events wouldn't have become a reality without this guy. Believe it."

"Is that so?" The daimyo of the Land of Flowers stood up. He bowed once to Naruto before going around the table in between them and walking over to Shikamaru's seat.

Shikamaru reflexively recoiled from the gentle-mannered boy's passionate march.

"And your name?" His voice broke shrilly over the last word in the sentence.

"Shikamaru," he replied slowly.

"Shikamaru! Thanks to you, my country was saved. Thank you so very much!"

The boy bowed his head with enough force to headbutt the still-seated Shikamaru right in the nose. Shikamaru pulled his head back to avoid a direct collision.

Eyes shining, the daimyo of the Land of Flowers took Shikamaru's hand in his own. "I heard all about you from Lord Ikkyu in the Land of Fire. He said that you fought together with Lord Naruto, that you are the Hokage's sharp and capable advisor."

The boy had made a stop in the Land of Fire before travelling on to Konohagakure. As soon as the continental summit had ended and war had been averted, this sedate, sober boy had announced to his retainers his intention to pay a visit to the Land of Fire and the village of Konoha. He'd insisted on the trip before any proper preparations could be completed. His visit to Konoha came seven days after the continental summit.

"I truly wished to meet you and express my thanks." Vigorously shaking the hand he still held up and down, the young daimyo bowed his head several more times.

"Uh, um," Shikamaru stammered.

"What is it?" Stars in his eyes, the boy pushed his face forward eagerly.

"There is something I very much wanted to ask you if I had the opportunity to meet you."

"Go ahead."

"Why didn't you speak at the continental summit? Why didn't you make a case for how irrational the Land of Earth was being to the daimyo of the world?"

"Ohh, is that it?" The daimyo of the Land of Flowers released Shikamaru's hand and pointed at himself. "What would the other nations think if a child with this sad little face pleaded his case in tears? The end result would have been the same had I voiced my complaints about the Land of Earth with a bold attitude and no tears. It's been six months since I became daimyo. The only remarkable result to come out of me speaking would have been the awkwardness of watching me flounder desperately. Ours is a small country. We don't have the necessary strength to defend ourselves. When I show weakness, that becomes the weakness of my own country. In which case, what should I do? I chose silence. As one of the countries directly involved, I said nothing and sat by quietly. By doing so, I was able to get through the summit without ex- posing any clumsy weakness. I decided to remain silent and leave the decision to the representatives of the world."

"So then you…"

"Naturally, I did discuss it with the retainers close to me, but the final decision was mine."

Precisely because his land was weak, he had decided to accept that weakness, acknowledge its reality, and work with that to the best of his abilities. The boy might have seemed out of his depth at first glance, but he had a solid core that would not break.

"Thank you so much for answering my impolite question." Shikamaru bowed his head.

"No, no." The daimyo of the Land of Flowers shook his head quickly from side to side. "It is I who must thank you so, so very much."

In the end, the boy bowed his head throughout the entire meeting, start to finish.

❖ ❖ ❖

Because he had left his official business undone, the daimyo of the Land of Flowers had decided to return home that very day. Naruto and Shikamaru went with him to the A-un main gates to see him off.

Shikamaru spotted his own son among the Konoha ninja who were guarding the retainers of the Land of Flowers encamped around the daimyo's driver. While Naruto and the daimyo chatted happily, he slid over to Shikadai on quiet feet.

"Cho-Cho, Inojin, you take the lead and keep an eye on the front. I'll go to the rear and watch the back," Shikadai was saying.

The three young ninja were in serious discussion, their faces pushed together. Their jonin supervisor Kazamatsuri Moegi watched over them from a step away. It appeared that the overall planning of the mission had been entrusted to Shikadai.

Moegi noticed Shikamaru's stealthy approach.

"So we'll go along like—Oh!" Shikadai looked back to get approval from Moegi and cried out when he noticed Shika-maru. The Land of Flowers people were moving forward with preparations for departure, and they all turned their eyes in this direction at the sound of this cry. "What's going on?"

"I could ask you the same thing," he said, grinning at the shocked look on his son's face.

"We'll be guarding them to the Land of Flowers," Moegi answered on Shikadai's behalf.

Guarding a daimyo was an important mission. Unless the village saw your team as competent and capable, you wouldn't be given a mission like this in the first place. It was proof of just how hard Shikadai and his team had been working. As a father, he couldn't help but smile.

"Hey, Shikadai!" He went to stand beside his son. "We might have dodged a war, but the Land of Flowers has got the world's attention now. We can assume all kinds of creepers are going to come out of the woodwork. The risk of the daimyo being attacked isn't zero. Don't let your guard down."

"I know."

Shikamaru had thought he would protest, but his son simply nodded in agreement. He was momentarily stunned at this docility, but made sure to maintain his composure so that no one would notice. He turned to Moegi. "The Anbu'll be accompanying you too, yeah?"

"Like, of course." A black shadow danced down next to Moegi.

It was a figure with a cat mask.

"Oh, so it's you, Hinoko."

"Gah! L-like, don't call me by my name in front of everyone!"

"Stop it," the monkey mask said, standing next to the cat.

"You're here too?" Shikamaru asked.

"The daimyo of the Land of Flowers is one of the principal actors in the continental summit," Ro declared. "It has been determined that two teams and eight people shall attend to him at this time."

"My eyes're, like, practically rolling out of my head at the thought of having to listen to more low-quality puns on the road again," Hinoko grumbled.

"Well, don't say that." Shikamaru smiled at her. "Other than those puns, Ro's a good ninja."

"L-Lord Shikamaru!" the older man protested. "What is the meaning of that?! Other than *those puns*?! Those puns themselves are the very essence of my being! No puns, no life!"

"So then quit being a ninja."

"That's, like, exactly right."

"Ngah! Who would punish a—"

Hinoko cut him off. "There's, like, a limit to how bad they can be."

"You weren't actually about to say 'punish a pun,' were you?" Shikamaru frowned doubtfully.

"It is strictly forbidden to ask, Lord Shikamaru!" The monkey threw his head back in indignation.

"Uh, um." Moegi shrugged apologetically.

Shikamaru popped his thumb up and pointed at the two Anbu. "However they look, these two have solid skills."

"What d'you mean, like, however we look?"

"Keep an eye on my son." Shikamaru told Moegi, ignoring Hinoko.

"Understood." Moegi nodded her head slightly.

"So, like, back to the mission," Hinoko said, and she and Ro bent at the knee for a jump.

Shikamaru remembered there was something he had to tell the two of them before they disappeared. "You both were a huge help again. Thanks."

"Do not hesitate to call upon us again in the future with any possible missions."

"We just, like, did what we had to."

The monkey and the cat disappeared into thin air.

"Shikadai," he called out to his son, who was talking with his comrades. "You don't know what's going to happen, but you know your own abilities. If you think the situation's too much for you, pull back. That's also a critical ninja skill."

Shikamaru wasn't talking down to his son here. If the boy rushed things and tried to do more than his abilities would allow for, his comrades would get hurt.

"I know," Shikadai replied, pursing his lips.

"Yeah? Okay, good luck out there then."

"It's a drag, but I'll go." His son grinned at him, but that easy smile told Shikamaru that Shikadai said the word *drag* in full understanding of what Shikamaru had told him the other day. "I'll be back in two or three days. Try not to fight with Mom while I'm gone."

"Shut up, you." Grinning, Shikamaru waved a hand at his son and then returned to Naruto and the daimyo.

Everyone who passed Shikamaru on the road stared at him.

This is embarrassing.

Red-faced, he hurried home. He had never once before walked along this street carrying something so over the top. As much as he tried, he couldn't ignore all the looks he was getting. But he had chosen this, so he couldn't complain. Even so, this was a bit much.

If he'd just bought the flowers at Ino's shop that time, it wouldn't have come to this—which reminded him, what had happened to those flowers? He figured Ino had probably sold them to someone else, but either way, he had done wrong by Ino. He'd have to apologize to her.

"That damned Naruto," he cursed, as he hid his face in the burden that filled his arms too full.

In that case, take home all the yellow ones!

It was only because of how kindhearted he was. Shikamaru knew that. Naruto hadn't meant anything bad. He really did know that. But he was so embarrassed at the moment, he could die.

His house came into view at last and his pace quickened.

Just a little farther.

He opened the front door and almost tumbled inside the house.

"You're home!" Temari came down the hallway to greet him, and her eyes grew wide when she saw him. "What is all this about?"

"Oh, uh." Still standing in the entryway, he looked away from her. "W-we sort of ended up helping the Land of Flowers a little, and so as thanks, the daimyo gave us a whole bunch of flowers. There were loads and loads, so I took a few."

"Only the yellow ones?" She looked at him doubtfully.

Shikamaru's arms were so full of yellow flowers, he could barely hold onto them all. In among the many different varieties, there also happened to be a certain flower that bloomed only in Sunagakure.

"You told me to make up for the anniversary thing, didn't you?"

Temari stared at him with serious eyes.

He held his breath, held the flowers, wondering if he'd offended her. Did she hate the idea of him making it up to her with secondhand flowers?

"Shikamaru."

"Y-yes?" Sensing an ominous aura, he waited for Temari to continue.

"Are you happy right now?"

"Hm?" He didn't really understand the question. He'd been utterly certain she would tear him to pieces, so this unexpected turn threw him for a loop.

"What do you think about life with us?" she pressed.

And now he realized what Temari was actually getting at. "Heh!" He laughed without meaning to.

Temari furrowed her brow angrily, her lips drawn tight.

"What do you think, looking at all this?" Still smiling, he held the flowers in his arms up toward her.

"Don't answer a question with a question." His wife glared at him.

"Thank you for everything."

"Ah!" For a moment, a gentle light shined in her eyes. She shook her head. Her hair, the same color as the flowers in full bloom, swung back and forth, and when she lifted her face again, her eyes had gone hard once again. "Shikamaru! Before you went to the Land of Iron, you left your shirt lying on the floor in your room! By the time I noticed it, it was about to stand up and walk away! I'm always telling you to put your laundry in the basket. How many times do I have to say it before you remember?!"

"S-sorry." A cold sweat sprang up on his forehead. "Um…"

"What?"

"Could you do something with these flowers?"

"Here." Temari opened her arms and leaned forward.

He handed over all of the yellow blossoms. "I'm sorry." He bowed his head neatly to his wife.

"Honestly." With a heavy sigh, Temari turned around and started to walk toward the kitchen. But she stopped after a few steps. Her back still turned to him, she said, "Thanks."

"S-sure thing," he replied.

His wife moved on brisk feet and disappeared into the kitchen.

Shikamaru took a deep breath and slowly exhaled. He sat on the step up into the house and pulled his shoes off. He had to remember to put his laundry in the laundry basket. Family was such a drag.

But…

"It's not too shabby."

The life Shikamaru wanted to protect was right here in front of him.

MASASHI KISHIMOTO

ABOUT THE CREATOR

Author/artist Masashi Kishimoto was born in
1974 in rural Okayama Prefecture, Japan. After
spending time in art college, he won the Hop Step
Award for new manga artists with his manga
Karakuri (Mechanism). Kishimoto decided to base
his next story on traditional Japanese culture. His
first version of *Naruto*, drawn in 1997, was a one-
shot story about fox spirits; his final version, which
debuted in *Weekly Shonen Jump* in 1999, quickly
became the most popular ninja manga in Japan.

TAKASHI YANO

ABOUT THE AUTHOR

Takashi Yano won the Shosetsu Subaru Newcomer Award
in 2008 with *Jashu*. He has published a number of works
as an expert on period dramas. In addition to the
Naruto novelizations *Shikamaru's Story* and *Itachi's Story:
Daylight/Midnight*, he is broadening the sphere of his work
with other novelizations, such as *Street Fighter*.